ANOMALOUS AFFECTIONS

ANOMALOUS AFFECTIONS

A Novel

Judith Ravenscroft

KARNAC

First published in English 2016 by
Karnac Books Ltd
118 Finchley Road
London NW3 5HT

British Library Cataloguing in Publication Data

A C.I.P. for this book is available from the British Library

ISBN-13: 978-1-78220-430-5

Typeset by Medlar Publishing Solutions Pvt Ltd, India

Printed in Great Britain by TJ International Ltd, Cornwall, Padstow

www.karnacbooks.com

To Timothy Hyman

PART ONE

MY LIFE WITH BELLE

WAITING

On a morning walk I paused at the top of the steps leading down to the canal to take in the view. It was the darkest time of the year. Trees and tangled undergrowth, the slick of water, all continued bleak. I walked along the towpath to the next bridge, crossed the canal, and returned on the opposite side. As I reached the foot of the steep path that led back up to the road, a black-clad figure emerged from the gloom and bore down on me, pressing forward like the masthead of a noble ship. His face was blank—skin and bones, empty of personality—and he had a doomlike air. But then, as he passed, this apparition looked searchingly at me, seeking and holding my gaze. I felt a spasm of fear but, with all the turmoil of Victor's departure, put the encounter out of my mind.

I saw Victor off at Heathrow. As we walked across a huge concourse crowded with passengers for the night flights, I burst into tears. It took me by surprise as much as it did Victor. I pressed my face to his chest so that people couldn't see me, and he hugged me as I tried to get a hold on myself and blubbered that I just felt emotional, and it was nothing he had to take seriously. I said the tears had come as a physical response to tension and didn't indicate a terrible sorrow, even if normally I wept rarely.

We sat in a restaurant and Victor ate something and we both drank tea. He looked at me keenly once or twice to see if I'd controlled my tears, or perhaps just to note the evidence of tears on my face. Soon, since there was nothing else to do, he decided to go through customs. I walked with him to the gate. We hugged, and he turned and walked off, and just as he reached the screen beyond which I wouldn't be able to see him I called his name and he turned to me. He looked bewildered, as if he couldn't understand what was happening, that he was going to America and I was not. He smiled wanly at me and then he was gone.

I turned away too and made for the exit, and as I walked along a tunnel towards the trains I began to cry again. I stopped and got out my glasses and put them on in the hope that they would hide my tears. In the train I opened my book (Constant's *Adolphe*) and began to turn the pages, taking in little. But by the time I got off at Kings Cross I was engaged enough to comprehend whole sentences.

That hadn't been the end of our parting. Soon after I got home, I was sitting at a loss in the living-room when Victor phoned from the airport to say that he felt as if he was going down with flu. There was a catch in his throat and he felt unwell and wondered if he ought to cancel the trip. I tried to encourage him, and later he told me that what I'd said, something about a few days' flu not being much in the context of a two-month trip, had helped him, but I felt upset that there was nothing I could do for him when he was on his own and distressed, and I asked myself how I could possibly have let him go off without me. I was pleased to hear his voice one more time, but when our conversation was over and I put down the phone, I wept again.

When I rang him the next day in California he sounded cheerful. His throat was troubling him, but not too badly. He had slept on the plane and arrived feeling better than when he left. He'd seen a doctor and was taking some pills. Now he was with his very good friends. I didn't know these friends, and I felt a tiny stab of jealousy. He'd forgotten his fears at the airport, while I had been living with them ever since. I was still here, in wintery London, in our flat in Finsbury, and he had moved there, thousands of miles to another continent, another time zone, another consciousness. I found it difficult to catch up with him, and perhaps he found it difficult, after the sudden transition, to recall what he'd left behind. But at least he'd arrived and was into the swing of things, and I could settle down to his absence.

That same evening, my friend Anna phoned to see how it had gone, Victor's departure, and how I was feeling. She asked me to visit her in the country, and I said I couldn't envisage leaving London. As I explained it to her, I thought I'd worry if I went away, about Victor, about the flat, about what might happen to both in my absence. Anna, who also found it difficult to leave home, for different reasons, understood my qualms but pointed out that she was on the phone and only an hour's train journey from London, so I could return quickly if I had to, as quickly as if I'd just gone to tea with a friend in south London. But not at night, I thought, which anyway missed the point; I wasn't worried about real possibilities but about ontological fears. Still, I wanted to see Anna, and for friendship's sake I would go.

An artist we knew had a private view of his work in a gallery in town. Victor had asked me to attend, and partly I did so for his sake, but I also wanted to test my resolve to live in the world while he was in America rather than hide myself away (as was my tendency)—even if private views were generally an ordeal for me.

When I got there I couldn't see anyone I knew and my one thought was to speak to the artist and leave. I refused a glass of wine, and began to make my way through the crowd. I kept having to apologise to people for getting in between them when they were talking, and then stepping sideways into someone else. Eventually I found myself at the edge of a group around the artist and waited for a chance to greet him.

For what seemed a long time, so that I became self-conscious, he resolutely avoided my eye, though I had the feeling he knew I was standing there. But then, as the person he was mainly talking to moved off, I stepped forward and he said hello. I told him Victor was away in America, and he said yes, of course, he'd known he was going, lucky man, and how he'd like to be there rather than here, anywhere rather than here, laughing. I said he seemed to be managing fine and it was a great show, though I'd have to return when it was quieter to see it properly. He thanked me, and then a gushy man interrupted to say how he must meet someone or other, and so I said goodbye.

Feeling relieved, I tried to look at the pictures. But as usual at such occasions I found it impossible to make much of the work. Either the crush forced me too close to the paintings, or if I stepped back people got in front of me. I continued to feel self-conscious, not wanting to snub anyone I knew, or on the other hand to look around me in case my eye met someone else's and I would have to greet them and would feel stuck to them, or would make them feel stuck to me.

On my way home on the bus I wondered why I'd made myself go to the private view which I'd been dreading all day. By now I should have developed the confidence to do what I wanted, to respect the way I was and live by it. It would have been good enough, and not discourteous, to see the pictures another time and send the artist an appreciative card.

I walked to work down the hill at the back of the house and then more or less in a straight line through Bloomsbury, finally taking a left turn into Soho. I was walking towards Russell Square one morning—spindly winter trees beneath a grey sky filled the space ahead—when a dark anger took hold of me. At that moment, a week or two into his absence, I felt abandoned by Victor. It seemed to me that he'd left me to do an unpleasant secretarial job, which I'd taken on because of our financial difficulties, to supplement my earnings from freelance work as an editor, and that somehow he'd managed to escape to America while I was left behind in my dreary, drudging existence. As I walked along a phrase kept repeating itself in my mind again and again: how could he do this to me, how could he do this to me, how could he do this to me.

Since ringing Victor just after he arrived in America I hadn't been able to make contact with him again. I knew which cities he was in and I knew the institutions he was lecturing at, but I didn't know where he was staying and so I hadn't been able to phone him. Later, he explained how difficult it had been, how he'd felt unable to ring long-distance from the private homes he was staying in and how he never had time to find a public phone because he was constantly being rushed by his highly organised hosts to the next appointment. For some reason I didn't, as I could have done, ring the institutions and track down the relevant person who could give me the phone number of the place where he was staying.

Before he left we had discussed my joining him for the Christmas holiday, and decided against it on the grounds of expense, wear and tear, and the difficulty of my fitting into his schedule halfway through. I thought it likely that I'd get there and he would have little time for me and so I'd hang about almost as alone as I was at home. I forgot these arguments as I walked round Russell Square, or at least as arguments they lost their force in the face of my anger and longing. But then, when it came to it, I didn't go, there was no point in going.

I finally spoke to Victor when he reached Denver, almost three weeks into his trip. I got through to him at once, and felt a catch in my throat as the familiar voice answered with a slightly impatient hello, as if he was in the middle of something and was irritated at being interrupted, and with his tone rising at the end into a question mark. "Hel-*lo?*"

"Hi," I replied, "it's me." And then, probably sounding a little histrionic, I said: "I can't go on not speaking to you." He seemed to laugh, unless what I heard was an intake of breath. I felt an enormous relief, to be able at last to hear his voice, so that I could place him in his hotel room in my imagination and he had some reality for me. No, he didn't look out on to a parking lot but on to ground that sloped down towards a frozen stream. He'd just come, he said, from having a swim in the pool. It was next to the place where people ate breakfast, idly watching the swimmers, on this occasion Victor and a small boy who splashed around a lot. It felt a little too public.

"A pool's a pool," I said, wondering whether it would have been the deciding factor in my joining him in Denver; if I'd known about the pool I might definitely have gone.

The hotel was nothing special, and noisy at night because his room was above a bar. "I tried to change it but there wasn't another one free."

"So if I'd joined you, we would have had a double and I'd have saved you from sleepless nights."

He laughed, uncertainly, as if he hadn't heard me, or hadn't got the point, but still picked up an edge in my voice and thought it safest not to inquire further. I asked if the sun was out, and it was and felt warm even though the snow was thick on the ground. That also sounded attractive to me, looking out of the window as I listened to him at a drizzly afternoon.

He told me what had been happening to him, about the friends he'd seen, and about the lectures, which had been going well apart from one in which the computer had crashed and he'd had to speak without showing any images, and how his throat was better, though his voice became hoarse during lectures, and how people had been kind and hospitable and welcoming. Then he asked about me, and I told him about Belle, and after a few affectionate words we said goodbye.

Belle was Isabelle de Charrière, the great *epistolière* of the eighteenth century. I had come to her by way of *Adolphe*,

Benjamin Constant's brilliant and disquieting story about a young man's seduction of an older, married woman, Ellénore, and her subsequent ruin and death. Adolphe tells how at first Ellénore resists his advances, but then succumbs, and how at the point of conquest his feelings begin to cool. He is too cowardly to tell her the truth, and when she leaves her husband and children for him, guilt and pity propel him into fleeing with her. He tries to do his duty by her, against the advice of his father and friends. Her recriminations turn inwards and, eventually, broken-hearted, she dies.

Ellénore's death was troubling. I couldn't see that aesthetics required such a harsh outcome, and I didn't entirely believe in Adolphe's declaration of anguish and guilt. I read in one source that Constant had based Ellénore on his old friend Isabelle de Charrière. Others insisted that the strongly individuated Belle bore little resemblance to his poor, compromised protagonist. Rather he may have had her in mind when, early on in his book, begun not long after Belle's death in 1805, Adolphe refers to the passing of an ageing woman whose exceptional intellect and tough morality powerfully influenced him at a young age. In any case, like others before me, I presumed to write a different ending for Constant's book.

Some friends rang from Holland to say they were coming to London for three days. I had never met this couple before but they were important friends, for I had corresponded with one of them for a couple of years as a result of some connection over writing. I felt nervous about their visit, handling it without Victor, as I generally let him take the lead at social occasions, while I held back; instead of taking responsibility, at least for my own friends, which I had done in the past, before Victor, but had since become lazy about.

I made an effort over dinner (chicken, fruit tart, cheese), taking some pleasure in it since I'd done no real cooking since Victor left. My friends brought wine and two pairs of thick, hand-knitted socks, for Victor and me, which were produced in the part of Holland they lived in. They laid themselves open with a generosity I did my best to match. Only one of them was Dutch; the other, the one I'd been writing to, Tom, was American. They lived quietly in a small town, where the Dutchman ran a research institute. They asked me about Victor, about how I was managing without him. I was pleased to be asked in such a simple, direct way, and to be able to explain it, and to have them listen to my explanation without interjecting too much with their own comparable experiences. How I defined it to them was that I missed Victor, in that I felt the lack of him, his absence, and counted the weeks until his return, yet at the same time I carried on more or less as usual, a normality that was partly that of my daily life at that time and partly my experience of solitude before I met Victor.

With the office closed for the holiday, I had a fortnight free to concentrate on Belle. I also arranged two or three fixed points of sociability, which were as much as I thought I wanted. I planned to write every day, but despite the perfect conditions—of which Victor's absence was one—it went badly. With every morning session I seemed to go through the motions, as if it was something to be done because it had to be, as a point of honour rather than because it engaged or enriched me, or sharpened my understanding, which was why I did it in the first place. I felt I'd lost my sense of aspiration, my fervour, so that when I wasn't sitting at my desk banging out a few desultory words I was lying on the daybed reading books chosen not for their distinction or even their relevance to my own project but because they held my attention, story books that relied heavily on suspense. I became aware that the hopes I'd begun this period of Victor's absence with, hopes to lead a full and directed life even if I missed him, threatened to give way to a sense of marking time, whereby I passed the days numbly and pointlessly until his return. It was as if I'd given up the struggle, and somehow this came to seem, in the days between Christmas and New Year, emblematic of my life in general. As if I had never found the stamina to keep on trying, and gave in too easily to discouragement. I felt humiliated by my mediocrity, a woman after all defined by a man, given meaning only by his presence.

Later I came to see the days around Christmas as marked mainly by their being at the fag-end of the year, so that whether Victor had been there or not I would have experienced much the same loss of direction. Even at the time I had the dim sense that these days, which might or might not have been better managed, were just bad days to be got through and that once the new year had started my mood would become lighter.

My brother Simon invited me over on New Year's Eve. His wife Alison had asked her sisters, with their husbands and offspring. By the time I got there the food had been reduced to little more than a mess of smeared plates as if the company had ravenously devoured every crumb of food. I was struck, as I stood by the table and took in the room, by the force and vitality of this family compared to my own, which was so much quieter, even languid. Victor's family too made this sort of impression on me, and it was as if we'd chosen partners, my brother and I, to supplement our own depleted sources of energy.

On my way home in a pre-ordered cab the driver asked me if I was going out to a party, and I said no, I was coming home from one. I laughed, but the driver seemed nonplussed. I asked him where he was from, and he said Zimbabwe; he had been in England for ten years, and had a university degree and a qualification in accountancy but had never been able to get a professional job. And so he drove a cab, and usually he took people to and from the airport, which was the journey he liked most because it reminded him that there was still a world outside England and one day he'd return to it. Soon, he said, there'd be an election in Zimbabwe and perhaps then the government would change and he could go home. All this had a chastening

11

effect on me, for what was the two months of my separation from Victor compared with the ten years this man had been parted from his family and forced to work in menial jobs? But I didn't want my feelings of optimism, now that the new year had begun, to be undermined by the driver's tragedy, and so I said little and looked out of the window. I saw that the streets were very busy, full of good-natured crowds, and it occurred to me that it had been unnecessary to order a cab, I would have been perfectly safe on the tube and would probably have enjoyed the sense of uproarious camaraderie. Then I felt badly about the driver and turned to him again, but he no longer wished to unburden himself.

When I got home I found a message from Victor on the answering machine and immediately rang him back in his hotel room. As I was to remember it later, this was one of the best calls we had while he was in America, not because of anything particular that was said, but because of the ease with which we spoke. It was as if he wasn't thousands of miles away in a place I could only imagine, and that we weren't in the outlandish circumstance of being separated for weeks on end, but as if we'd seen each other only a day or two before, and would again shortly, and meanwhile we were passing the time of day. But we ended on a wistful note with the realisation which came quite suddenly towards the end of our conversation that we missed each other and it would be several more weeks before we were together again, assuming we would be; a rider I felt obliged to add, in my mind, not out loud, but like a good-luck charm, so as not to tempt fate.

I went to see Anna in the Kentish countryside. We took a long walk, setting out from her back door and making a great circle to end up at her front door. We walked round the edges of turfy fields, across heath-lands strewn with cow pats, through straggly copses; and we crossed a stream, jumping from one stone to another. It was as exhilarating in its way as a long walk in London, because of a feeling of unity with my surroundings, but without the particular sense in London of continuity with past generations of Londoners, which conferred a sort of immortality.

We talked about a book we had both read, a diary kept by an older woman, in her sixties, in a remote part of New England, where conditions through the winter were severe, with dangerous wildlife as well as deep frosts and wild storms, and she was constantly fighting a desperate loneliness, although she couldn't imagine living in any other way. I admired her, for her courage in being true to her reclusive character, even if it was a lifelong difficulty, and for the intensity of her concentration in every aspect of her life. Anna said that in her experience it was impossible to be reclusive in the country because every Tom, Dick, and Harry—none of them a soulmate—were forever barging in, and her concentration was continually undermined by her fear of crisis, or by actual crises, failures in the system brought on by inclement weather.

My back ached after such a long walk, my legs were tired, and Anna commented on my unfitness.

Later, we sat in front of a fire, which was a comfort against the threatening sounds of a wild night, and it felt good to be there with Anna, who was such a very good friend. But even so I felt restless and melancholy, anxious about my home, in case something was wrong there, more than about Victor, who seemed so far away, even more so because I myself was away from home, that I could barely conjure him in my mind.

It was on my way home from Anna's that I saw Belle's house. It appeared in the darkening valley below, so unexpected and so fleeting in its fragile, whitish elegance that it might have been a ghost, no sooner seen than lost as the bus plunged into a tunnel of trees. But then it came into view again, looming above us, on its solitary knoll. A house with a haunting beauty, perfect in its generous proportions, its soft pale pinkish stone, its wide-eyed windows that drew one in despite the drawn blinds, the closed gate, the darkness. I knew I would give it to Belle, never mind that it was in Kent, not Switzerland, and of a later time. I imagined dust sheets on the furniture, field mice running across bare wooden floors, an abandoned house, or a house that someone would come back to, that Belle would come back to, never to leave again.

In the days before Victor's return I tried to finish what I was writing (about Belle's first meeting with Constant in Paris; there was some mystery about why she had gone there, alone, without her husband, whom she seems to have left abruptly). I wasn't writing it for Victor and his being there or not was irrelevant to its completion. Partly I was just making a deadline to galvanise myself, but I also felt a strong desire to complete what I had worked on while Victor was away, to be able to draw a line underneath his absence and everything to do with it.

The day before his return a delicate grey light signalled, if not the end of winter, at least the possibility of spring. Descending the hill at the back of the house to walk into town, I felt elated, taken out of myself, and threw my head back to offer my face to the gentle air—until I started to topple over, as if unbalanced by a tug from behind. Returning to consciousness, I was able to right myself.

The streets were quiet at that hour, in the early afternoon; the houses, pairs of stucco villas, appeared abandoned, their windows staring blankly, and I passed no one until reaching the main road at the foot of the hill. There, cars hurtled past as I waited at the lights, but pedestrians were few until I reached the streets around the university. Now I was no longer taken up by the light and the air, but took note of the people, their faces, tense, self-absorbed, their bodies pressing forward as mine did, occupying its space and respecting that of others with an intuition based on long experience. Only the tourists got in the way, unsure of themselves, of where they were going, lacking any sense of their own rhythms as well as others', children in the ways of London.

A friend, Alice, was waiting for me under the portico of the British Museum. As we embraced I felt myself stiffen, become unsteady, again as if I might topple, and shuffled my feet.

Alice asked: "What is it?"

"I'm just a bit stiff." I easily steadied myself, and shrugged off my sense of an alien force.

Victor was due back very early on a Saturday. On the Friday evening I went to bed at ten in order to be up by six-thirty in the morning. But I woke every half-hour through the night, and at last got up and made a pot of tea and had drunk it by the time I heard a taxi outside and going to the window saw Victor. And it was as if he was returning as he so often had before from a few days up north, until I opened the door and we hugged and I buried my face in the unfamiliar smells of another country.

A FATE LIKE LEAD

One early summer's day we walked, Victor and I, to the river, taking the street that curved with generous swathes down the hill from the Angel to Smithfield. Past St Paul's, we went down the steps to the riverside, where we stood at the balustrade, looking up and down stream and across to the old power station, which had become the Tate gallery, on the south bank. The water was still and grey, like the sky, and the view was big and wide, a great expanse of greyness, but pearly, pinkish, purply too.

We took a taxi home because I was troubled by an aching back.

My back almost stopped me going with friends on a long walk across the Heath. But the day was glorious—a sun you could feel on your back, a world that sparkled—and I wanted only to be out in it. We started in Highgate, walking down past the allotments into Kenwood, and across to Parliament Hill. Long before we halted for coffee I wanted to lie flat on the ground.

A friend lagged behind with me and asked what it was, this bad back, as if he didn't quite believe in it, it didn't correspond to what he knew of bad backs.

"And you're walking oddly," he said, but couldn't define how it was. It was different, he said, it had changed. Perhaps I wore ill-fitting shoes?

At an exhibition of paintings, one image made a particular impression on me, a charcoal drawing of a man about to enter a cave. The black tones gave a certain ambiguity to the feeling of the man, who seemed both eager and fearful in relation to the cave, which perhaps he wasn't going to enter, because the dream, which was what the image felt like, would stop before he had to. If that had been my dream, I thought, I would have felt an inevitability about entering the cave, in which apprehension and curiosity and resignation were all mixed up.

And what with one thing and another I fell over, tripped, and couldn't save myself, or lost my balance—afterwards I couldn't reconstruct the circumstances, but remembered the cracking sound of bone on concrete as my knees hit the floor and the feeling that my whole world had given way.

A friend, mainly of Victor's, though I liked her too, had a birthday, and someone we didn't know gave a party for her. As the weeks passed and the date of the party came closer, I became agitated at what I had let myself in for. It became an enormous obstacle in my path, something I had to get past before I could regain my composure. I counted the weeks and days and hours until it would be over and I imagined how that would be, when we got home from the party, and I had survived it, how I'd lie in bed beside Victor, how relieved I'd feel, and we'd talk about what it had been like and then read a little before going to sleep.

We expected a real party, with more people than could sit round a table, enough people so that I could sit in a corner with just one, or if not, then at least I could leave after a couple of hours without anyone minding, rather than having to stick it out through two or three courses and coffee. But when I walked into the house and glanced into the dining room I saw at once that the round table had been laid for ten people. I looked at Victor, who wouldn't meet my eye, and I felt an acute stab of betrayal, whether by Victor or his friend or life I couldn't say. And then, though it wasn't too bad, because most people try to be friendly, and it's rare to meet a truly obnoxious person, it wasn't too good either, because I had very little to say to any of these people, who were from another world of business and banking, or if I did (and it's not impossible that if I'd been trapped in a lift with any one of them I would have got quite far) I couldn't say it with other people listening—which is the problem with dinners for a few people, that you're expected to sing for your supper and feel ashamed if you don't. As it was, I kept losing the drift of the conversation, and sat as if struck dumb, and fearful lest someone require an opinion from me on whatever they were talking about, which had invariably escaped me.

The other person who wasn't having a very good time was our friend whose birthday it was. She looked as if she had wandered into the party by mistake, someone else's birthday party, and was baffled by the attention she was getting. Baffled too, the other guests and our hosts stopped attending to her, and mostly, like me, she sat in silence. Later, she told Victor she had taken some comfort from my presence, since I too seemed at a loss. She said that she'd wanted to laugh when I reached out to pick some grapes from a bowl of fruit at the centre of the table and then abruptly withdrew my hand as if I'd realised I wasn't supposed to eat the grapes, that they were there for display.

Sometimes I found myself blaming Victor for involving me in social occasions with people I had nothing to say to, and he'd defend himself: you never knew when you might meet a new friend and if you didn't go to parties you never would; that conversation helped to clarify your views about things; that even if the talk seemed pointless it got you closer to the people you were talking to.

"You'd do better," he advised me, "to think about how other people strike you, rather than worrying about the impression you're making on them." And: "Let people know who you are instead of shutting yourself up."

This time he agreed with me that it was a pointless occasion. And I had to agree with him: the futility of the party was unusual, something neither of us could have anticipated, and that we had both felt obliged to support our friend on her birthday and could hardly have refused. In the course of a life, Victor said, a person has to expect a few bad evenings.

He painted a picture which seemed to show how it was for me. He was leaping on to a bus, grabbing the pole with one hand to hoist himself on to the platform. Not everyone noticed the floundering figure on the right, the hesitant, fearful woman who wasn't sure whether she wanted to follow him, whether she had the courage to make the leap, and was weighing up the dangers, and obviously envisaging disaster: as he flew through the air she saw him fall, caught up in the wheels of the bus, mangled and dead. And he wanted her to follow.

Stiffness in my limbs, unsteadiness, a back that refused to get better. And a peculiar way of walking which neither I nor Victor nor anybody else could describe except in terms of its unfamiliarity. Later, someone would tell me that a normal gait was an even gait; that however a person might walk, each side was the same, and that I walked unevenly, as if I was two people, split down the middle. But at the time neither I nor anyone I asked could define what was odd about my walking. So I watched people in the street and walked behind them trying to imitate their walk, though I knew this to be futile, since everyone walked differently, and it was my own particular way that I had lost and wanted to regain, along with a state of thoughtlessness about walking as I made my way about London. Also, Victor commented that I kept saying how clumsy I was with my hands. I felt bound to challenge Victor's depiction of my fearfulness, but I wondered silently about the pain in my deepest places, like a jagged ache through the root of me, coming two or three times and then not again.

I had a theory of my own. A young man visited, the son of a friend, who had come to London to study. He told me about the course he was doing, that once he'd completed it and had a qualification then all sorts of doors would open for him. He'd get a job which would pay for a flat in town so that he wouldn't have to commute from the suburb he was living in now. He was full of optimism, in the way of people at the beginning of something new, especially if they're young.

As I was talking to him, I remembered a newspaper article I'd read about a young woman who had chosen to remain celibate and at twenty-six wrote a book about it. Celibacy, it seemed, was no longer something to be ashamed of as it had been in the days when it was called virginity and one didn't choose it. It seemed that lots of men had wanted to sleep with this young woman but she'd held off. And that, I thought, would make it much easier, to be able to boast of one's strength of character rather than admit to failure on the sexual front. I didn't say any of this to the young man (later I thought that if I had we might have had a more interesting conversation). It just passed through my mind as he spoke of his plans, perhaps because of the boy's optimism, his easy assumption that he'd find the job and flat he wanted, just as the young woman in the newspaper article seemed to know what she wanted to do and to do it. Perhaps that's what connected them in my mind, their youthful confidence, and my envy, an ageing woman's envy of the young.

That gave me one clue. A dream seemed to provide another: I'm standing pressed against a tree as if hiding. Voices call me. I know what they have to tell me, I've seen what was coming: my mother's struggle as she gasped for breath. I know and don't want to hear it said out loud. So I press one ear against the knobbly bark and with my hand cup the other. Even as I stand there, I think that I can't remain clamped to that tree forever. Next, an open door and, in the room beyond, a window ablaze with sunlight. I enter and see a young woman lying naked on the bed. Smooth skin, pure lines, limbs askew with a child's awkwardness—and dead.

"That's not my mother!" I say in the knowledge that this isn't the body of a woman who has carried children but a girl's that has borne none.

Someone brushes past with a jug of water and a towel, and begins to wash the corpse. Smooth, delicate hands go about their work. Under my eyes, they become red and rough, and marked, like my own hands, by the blemishes of age. Later, I would give this dream to Belle, when in her disconsolate middle age I imagined her thoughts returning to her mother's death. Its meaning seemed obvious: we were burying our youth and suffering the first infirmities of old age.

Months passed. The hot summer gave way to a sweetly melancholy autumn. I sat on a bench in the garden of our square and lapped up the sun, knowing that soon we'd get no warmth from it for months to come. The anxiety that had settled on me seemed to be in abeyance. I believed my aches and pains to be nothing but a temporary stage of life. All was well—but then, on my way home one evening, walking along Theobald's Road, I again encountered the apparition that months before had passed me on the canal—the same masklike face, neither young nor old, neither ugly nor handsome. Again he seemed to emerge out of a dim and misty gloom. He stared at me, and I felt unsettled and tried to avoid his eye.

Next, an old acquaintance telephoned and said, "I heard you were sick." His words shocked me. I wanted to protest his misinformation, as if it hadn't occurred to me, as apparently it had to others, that I was ill. In bookshops, surreptitiously, I began to look for a label for my ailments but couldn't find them exactly described. A doctor supplied it, after journeying round my body with the fluency of a musician practising his instrument. Moving on from one part to the next, no pauses, but a continuous, concentrated proceeding: eyes, mouth, arms, legs, extremities—he peered, tapped, manipulated, and pronounced: Parkinson's disease.

What I remember now of the days and weeks that followed has little feeling. It's as if the shock of it numbed my memory, so that though I can see myself doing what I did, and hear myself saying what I said, I don't feel what I felt.

I remembered a fancy of my mother's. As a young woman, looking out of a window of her childhood home, she had seen a large young girl with her chin in the air like a camel, loping towards her across the street. Years later, suddenly (while sitting in the waiting room of a dentist in the same street), she remembered the girl and believed she recognised her as me. "You came from the future," was how she had put it, laughingly, but it always made me uneasy. If the future can appear in the past, and since as we all know the past can resonate in the future, then there was no escape: as she lay dying I knew without a doubt that my mother expected me soon to follow her. As I approached her bed, I felt the force of her will, the draw of her charisma, and it took every mite of my strength to resist her. She would not be patient, she was biding her time only until my spirit was weak, and then she would call me.

I watched myself closely. Through that winter and into spring I always walked the same daily route to the canal and back so as to note any change in the time I took, how breathless I became while climbing the steep hill up to the road from the water, how tired I felt when I got home. Sometimes I was slow and listless, and at other times I took a minute or two less and felt well at the finish. There seemed to be no pattern, or steady deterioration.

People go on, the doctor had said, for ten years. Or fifteen. Even twenty. Before what? Death? Before the condition became severe? Victor and I thought of the friend who was dying in those days, how grateful he'd be for ten years. Ten years was a long time. A decade. It was unimaginably longer than six months, say. And perhaps there'd be more.

I sought information but then found I couldn't bear to read it. In the library I looked out the famous essay in which Dr Parkinson described the disease his name was given to.

It made harrowing reading and I got no further than page four ("its last stage … the wished for release") before fleeing.

Then, there were other people, those whose response seemed to me inadequate, because they said too much or not enough, or nothing at all, were too empathetic or insufficiently so, though what I wanted I had no idea, and perhaps when someone made the right response it was just chance. There were also the people I believed had done me down, the "I'll show them" people, the snubbers and dismissers, the jeerers and sneerers. Now, with my mind's eye, I saw pity in their faces, pity tinged with triumph.

I came to believe it had always been within me, the malady: a stickiness in manner and mind, a lack of stamina, episodes of clumsiness and inarticulacy, all of which, slowly, over many years, grew and coalesced until they ceased to be qualities of being and became signs of disease. It seemed important to be able to trace its origins to the distant past, to look for clues in a place and time that were beyond my influence. I dreamt that a young girl tugged at my arm for attention. She put her mouth to my ear to tell me her name, which wasn't the usual sort of name but consisted of a sentence of several words. I immediately forgot her words, either in the dream or when I woke, but clearly she had something to tell me, something I needed to know.

I dug out a photo of the child I once was: standing ankle deep in the shallows of a sea, hands on hips, head held to one side, eyes squinting in the sun. It brought a memory of youthful grace. My eyes fixed wide, I see the sandy seabed arranged in elegant swathes, dappled with gentle ridges; and dead-white as if boneless hands, mine, cutting through the limpid water. I reach upwards, kicking my legs hard, arms outstretched above my head to break the surface, an elegant streak cutting cleanly through the water, and causing hardly a ripple.

I looked again at the photo of my child self. For what? Signs of illness, or frailty? or defiance and resilience? It told me nothing. One night, I lay flat out, trancelike, feeling my arms and legs as blocks of wood in which the forms of my limbs were only faintly suggested. I experienced myself as a tiny kernel encased in an alien body. I knew that if I moved I could break the spell, but wanted to see where it took me, this fullness and rigidity, this absence of subtle variation. It took me nowhere, allowing me no redemptive hallucinations, passing off of its own accord, so that shapeliness was restored to me. The episode brought a phrase to mind, one that I'd just read in a story by Büchner, and now repeated to myself again and again: a fate like lead, a fate like lead, a fate like lead.

MY BELLE

PORTRAIT: Reddish hair, high colour, wide open faces: the parents, cousins, are of a kind, their children shaped in the same mould. The mother, at one end of the table, smiles indulgently, at no one in particular. The father, at the other, appears to think only of chewing. Neither takes any notice of two young boys who, on and off their chairs, are teasing a cat, though an older sister looks their way and may soon restrain them. An adult son sits beside his mother and raises a glass to his lips. And, next to the father, a young woman we know to be Belle laughs challengingly at the brother who's her favourite. This is Ditie, and from his place down the table he seems to look up at Belle, at the centre of the picture, their star. Her gifts are prodigious; by now (she is nineteen), as well as being fluent in French and her native Dutch, she has learnt English, translated Horace from Latin, studied mathematics, made music, written poems and many letters—and is composing her first novella. She is said to be a beauty, but here what is notable is her liveliness, and an almost quivering sensitivity—excitement, anticipation—in the curves of her profile.

D'HERMENCHES: Belle met d'Hermenches in The Hague, at a ball at the Duke of Brunswick's. He wore a black band round his head, for reasons unknown. He was famous for it, so nobody bothered to explain what it was for, whether it was just an idiosyncratic accessory, or he believed it helped his chronic headaches. He would have made an impression, even without his reputation—as a soldier and man of letters, and as a rake. It was also said that he was a friend of Voltaire.

He stood alone, detached, watching the crowded room with aplomb. Belle seized her chance and introduced herself. "You're not dancing, sir?"

"I've never learnt to dance and talk at the same time. And I prefer to talk—when I can find anyone to engage with me."

"That's just how I feel about it."

"Yes, I noticed how you worked your way across the room. You must have greeted twenty people—and apparently found no one to your liking."

"I haven't got time to waste."

"But you have a lifetime. Look at me. I'm more than halfway through and still stand about watching the world. You're in too much of a hurry."

"Holland isn't the world, it's a backwater where you're amusing yourself for a few days as a researcher might. It's not the world for me either, but it's almost the only part of it I've seen and I know it far better than I want to."

"And when you catch sight of a stranger across the room you make a point of going over to him."

"I'm told you're a friend of Voltaire."

"Ah—you admire him?"

"Not his new book. It's a potboiler."

"Is that what they say here?"

"I have no idea what they say here. I myself think it's a potboiler."

"You're wrong. It's a difficult book, misunderstood by those who are prejudiced against him."

26

"What kind of argument is that? To say I'm wrong because I hold a different opinion from you. To call me prejudiced because I disagree with you."

She didn't like the way he laughed, that he was apparently laughing at her, and she turned to leave. He took her arm to hold her back, and in the course of the evening he offered something—friendship, or a correspondence, it's not clear exactly what, but she understood he wanted to continue their exchange. Then she didn't hear from him. Several weeks went by, and rather than let him go she again made the first move.

"I will not dissemble," she began her letter—but then did. She was writing because she'd failed to seek him out to say goodbye, and believed in observing the courtesies. She expected no answer, indeed urged him to burn her silly, girlish note; but, on the other hand, she would hate him (no less) if he failed to honour the trust she was placing in him. Hadn't he claimed to want her confidence?—he had said he desired it ardently—and she reminded him too of his promise to be sincere, his assurance that she had nothing to fear from him.

And then, having dared, and elicited a response, she lost her nerve, wanted to call a halt to the whole thing. D'Hermenches, at thirty-seven, was seventeen years older than her. Perhaps someone, possibly her brother Ditie, told her that the sickly wife he left at home in the country was not the mother of the daughter who sometimes travelled with him. Belle came clean: she risked her reputation, already there were rumours, potential husbands would be put off.

He replied with some memorable phrases: "the blaze of my friendship", "the affinity of our souls". And what kind of suitors were these, he wanted to know, that they objected to her corresponding with the one person capable of appreciating her genius?

She wrote one more letter, and then another—and felt ridiculous, threatening to stop writing to him even as she continued.

So she withdrew her objections and they settled into it. Supreme practitioners of the epistolary art, ardent students of the human condition, over fifteen years they opened up their lives and thoughts one to the other, for their own delight and ours.

MARRIAGE: She didn't want to talk about marriage, she wrote to d'Hermenches, but when he pressed her she admitted she needed a husband because only then could she be free. She wanted to live without constraints, at liberty to study and write what she pleased, to choose her own friends, to educate her children. She couldn't do this on her own—it would distress her parents—and her husband must willingly give her her head.

D'Hermenches, a fixer by nature, came up with the marquis. What he seemed to have in mind was a threesome. He envisaged their perfect happiness—not just hers and the marquis's but his own too, as if he'd be marrying her by proxy.

Just in time, she discovered passion, or its absence. Away from the marquis she imagined the one, and when she was with him, which occurred rarely, she experienced the other. She blamed herself, she said to d'Hermenches: she was awkward, clumsy. But his friend's pursuit of her was altogether too tepid for a woman who felt her chastity as a deprivation. She wanted to hear no more about husbands, if she needed one she'd find him herself.

Then her mother died. They had all questioned the inoculation—Belle's father, the doctor, her older brother Eric—but Belle's certainty, her contempt for their ignorance, her youthful embrace of what was new, had overborne their doubts. Only her mother trusted her in the matter of the cowpox—and died of the fever that resulted. And Belle's father blamed her. Possibly. It's been suggested. And to me seems likely.

After the burial her father was inconsolable. He glanced up at Belle when she entered the room, his expression distracted,

28

as if he hardly knew her, and at once turned away. Eric stood behind him, and taking his cue from his father also ignored her. Instinctively she looked to Ditie for reassurance—he opened his eyes wide, and she nodded slightly in response.

She walked over to her father, placed a hand on his shoulder, and when he looked up bent to kiss his forehead. He gestured, as if to say, yes, yes, but not now—and returned to his contemplation of the fire.

He didn't invite her, as the oldest daughter, to take her mother's place at table. Belle sat in her usual seat beside him until it occurred to her to move down the table and busy herself with her sister's children. One refused to eat and while Belle coaxed him the other gave morsels of food to the cat under the table. The cat jumped on to the child's lap and from there to the table. Their father looked up and gazed bewildered at the animal. Then, as he turned to Belle, his head jerked in a spasm—of what? It was more than irritation. But surely he didn't hate her.

She took the children to visit her old nurse, wife of a harbour master on the coast. She walked beside the sea and, drenched by the waves, waited beneath vast, racing skies for her spirits to lift. But even the sea couldn't break the hold of her depression. She was there as carer to two young children, in conversation most of the day with them or her nurse. If she was going to be confined, let it not be as unwilling companion to a grieving and judging widower, in a home and world that imprisoned her.

D'Hermenches knew Charles de Charrière of old, came from the same corner of Switzerland. "An excellent man, but ..." He didn't list his failings, nor did Belle press him. They had books in common, which seemed good enough for her, even if Charles, her brothers' tutor, couldn't match her gifts and knew it: he wrote that he was like her pupil, that she made him forget his role as sage. Belle would continue to refer to him as the tutor long after he ceased to be one.

Charles's doubts were shared by d'Hermenches. Belle was attaching herself to a man who would always remain in her shadow and would come to resent it. And she, having soon exhausted anything that was interesting or surprising in him, would look in vain for stimulating relationships among his friends and neighbours. She had misunderstood her needs and was too impatient. All she thought of was getting out of her father's backwater. Couldn't she see that by marrying Charles she would simply plunge into another? Aged thirty, she could expect another thirty years in which to enjoy or endure her choice, "and thirty years is a very long time".

She hesitated. But then wrote to him to explain: after losing her mother she hadn't wanted to marry. But her family liked Charles, and so did she; he was a sincere and reasonable man, and he loved her without illusion. Besides, she was in an awkward situation at home. She could see no other way of changing it. And so she'd told her father she was ready to sign the contract that would formally engage her.

They had to curtail the honeymoon because of a condition she called her vapours, perhaps because no doctor was ever able to define it: a recurring indisposition, or perhaps a cyclical lowering of spirits. Her health would always bother her, but, instructed by her sisters-in-law, she found she liked domestic tasks and became expert at washing the household's linen—news that d'Hermenches must have received with disgust. Otherwise the main difference from her previous life, she wrote to him, was that she no longer always slept alone. Thus, she had settled into her new home, and declared herself delighted.

MADAME DE CHARRIERE: I'm taller than her, and thinner—wrote Charles, of Belle. She's fair and I'm dark. She speaks fast and holds nothing back. I prise the words out of myself and rarely manage more than a sentence at a time. In a foreign language, she becomes the part, throwing herself into look and gesture, as well as perfectly mimicking the sounds of the words, while I'm unable to be anyone but myself.

I love walking, but she hates it. She huffs and puffs and thrashes her way through the woods so you can hear her coming at a hundred yards. I walk fast for a short distance, and then I'm tired. She walks complainingly but can, if she must, keep going for many hours.

She's usually warm, whereas I feel the cold. Even in summer I often need a coat, but she casts hers off with the first signs of spring.

She drinks a great deal of coffee, and likes strong red wine. I take a small glass of spirits after dinner for my health, and only the weakest tea. I eat fish, soup, vegetables. She prefers roast meats and strong sausage and has a passion for apricots.

I sleep better than she does. When she's awake she endlessly jackknifes as if clinging to a raft that's being tossed about on a rough sea.

She loves the theatre, and I don't: I feel confined and restless, but she laughs and weeps and shouts bravo at the end so that people turn to stare.

She goes through the journals quickly and untidily, so that I have to put them back in order before I can read them.

Departures make her anxious but she loves arrivals; when she reaches her destination all her dread gives way to excitement. Away, I do exactly what I do at home. While she rushes round seeing everything, I stay in my room waiting impatiently for her return. Nor am I a sightseer at mealtimes; she eats whatever she's never eaten before.

She hates the return, finds the house uncongenial, the countryside bleak, and feels trapped and lonely. And though she rarely sits and stares out of the window, or hesitates when asked to account for her day, since she always has a pile of books to read, letters to answer, neighbours to receive, sometimes it's as if fear catches up with her: she goes to bed with mysterious symptoms, pulls the blankets up over her face, refuses all medicines and comfort until—as suddenly as she succumbs, she recovers, jumps out of bed, throws open the windows, and runs through the house as if astonished to be alive ...

Those words are mine, in fact, not Charles's. Increasingly, I found myself drawn to the gaps in Belle's story, episodes that were suggested but in detail could only be guessed at; not her life so much as how I imagined the parts of it that were lost to us. Such as the matter of her childlessness: I was tempted to give her a phantom child, but there's no reason to believe she conjured one, except in the offspring, often fatherless, of protagonists in her novels.

As d'Hermenches had predicted, Belle soon became bored in the small Swiss town near Neuchâtel. She wrote little other than letters (the first great correspondence of her life was over, the second yet to begin) and gave herself over to daily life—with increasing impatience at its banalities. In one account she sits surrounded by guests but speaking to no one. Her silence and her scowling face attracted their glances but warned them to keep their distance.

The pastor said something witty. Well he might. If she could have tolerated his cynicism he might have been a friend for her.

"What did you say?" Belle called, jumping up.

"We're speaking of the joy a virtuous person brings both to himself and to those around him."

"Only an unvirtuous person could claim such a thing."

The pastor, naturally, was taken aback; she could see she interested him. What had he said to Charles?—that she revealed herself more than she realised.

"Virtue in the sense you mean it—sticking to a list of pointless rules with stubborn imperviousness—is an hypocrisy: it makes a misery of the person who flaunts it, and he makes misery for everyone else."

"And you, how would you define it?"

"It's living as you want and doing the work you were born for."

The pastor's wife raised her voice: "There's no contradiction between virtue and misery, or rather, perhaps, happiness doesn't by definition follow from virtue, though it might."

"My dear,"—the pastor—"you're always so moderate, a devotee of the middle way, whereas Belle and I are extremists."

Belle didn't like this at all, either being claimed by the pastor as a kindred spirit or the snub he dealt his wife. She turned her back to them, picked up the teapot, and moved restlessly among her guests to fill their cups.

The years passed, still she wrote little—until something roused her, perhaps closure of the long and debilitating search for fertility, then the panicked realisation that she'd been waiting for her life to begin when in fact it was already half over. In desperation, she produced three short epistolary novels in a row. Championing the cause of women who in one way or another are at odds with the staid and convention-bound world they inhabit—an unhappy wife, an unmarried mother, a young girl humiliated by the search for a husband—they incriminate the tyrannical authority of stupid, insensitive men. Every citizen of Neuchâtel saw himself pictured in her books, which brought her local fame and notoriety.

FRACTURE: They would walk. That had already been decided, as an economy and to do themselves good. They walked in silence because otherwise they would bicker. In any case Belle, come straight from her desk, hadn't yet freed her mind of the day's writing and was rehearsing her sentences. Charles thought of a woman with a great nest of hair, its curls and ringlets like a golden haze round her long pale face. Turning a corner, they were suddenly in a crowd, and Belle felt her stomach tighten with nerves. Were all these people heading for the concert? So many she would have to greet and name one to another. She began to rehearse the names of those she knew would be there but then stopped at the futility of it.

"There was a sigh," Charles said, not unkindly.

"Are all these people on their way to hear Ragrid?"

"Who knows who they are—does it matter? Anyway, you like to get lost in a crowd."

"That's true."

"But do try to be civil to anyone we know."

"Have you ever known me not civil?" Belle turned on him so abruptly that a pin sprung from her hair, out of the knot she hadn't rearranged for the occasion. She let it go, and Charles moved ahead as if—she thought—to distance himself.

She noticed Colette, come from Lausanne, had her eye fixed on Charles's retreating back and might have been trying to catch him up until she caught sight of Belle and quickly smiled and waved. There was a muddle: as they embraced Colette's famous hair got caught in Belle's sleeve. Charles came back to disentangle them, and Colette, laughing shrilly, went careering up the steps into the village hall. Charles watched her go with a sort of flustered complacency. Suddenly, Belle understood, a spark of intuition, and with it came the searing pain of humiliation.

Charles scraped the plate with his knife, wiped the knife with the lump of bread he'd been kneading with the fingers of his left hand, and then ate the doughy result. As his fingers deposited the morsel in his mouth he looked towards the window, and didn't notice that Belle shuddered as his fleshy lips closed on the bread. Slowly he chewed it. Then he swallowed, and glanced at her as if he'd sensed her disgust and was challenging her to express it.

Unless he was simply oblivious of his actions, distracted by wariness—as he had always been wary of her brilliance, and how much more so now, with the shame—or in defiance—of having broken his marriage vows to her. He looked towards the window again as if it might offer a means of escape.

"Are you going to Lausanne?" Her voice was harsh, and made him flinch. He stared at her with surprise—or was it distaste for her crudeness? Perhaps he was simply afraid of her cutting words.

She sat back, lolled almost, and jeered: "But I should be grateful to you."

"Grateful?"

"For making my position so clear to me."

"Your position is exactly what it's always been. You're my wife …"

"Exactly. And you are my husband."

He couldn't follow her into the treacherous waters of her sarcasm. He faltered, looked away, but not, this time, towards the window.

She leant across the table. Suddenly she was intense, almost hissing the words in her haste to expel them. "I don't blame you, you know. My own case is no less despicable."

"I've always esteemed you. Your gifts—"

"Of course."

"I offered you an escape."

"From my family? Oh yes, and freed me from the unspeakable humiliation of looking for a husband. Don't mistake me, Charles. I'm grateful. You have exposed my hypocrisy. But how can I live with it?"

"Live with what? I've told you it's over."

"Live with my error. Mine."

An error that wouldn't have occurred if for once in her life she'd listened to the advice of others. Or probed her feelings instead of attending only to the logic of her mind which had entirely convinced her of the sense of it: marriage to the tutor.

At last their eyes met, and she found herself unable to look away. What did he see? Her customary disdain, perhaps. Or the blank incomprehension of a trapped creature before it's found the strength to flee.

NEVER AGAIN

*A*daily walk round the square. The circumnavigation. Never mind how. Shuffling would do—until, all of a sudden, I'm on the tips of my toes and breaking into a run, hurtling forwards, and clutching at the railings in an attempt to halt my mad rush.

Not to trip and fall, anything but that trickster's joke, played by my body in league with a god of slapstick. Only concentrate. The usual drill—heels to ground, a deep breath, then, balanced, let go, stand, think about walking, one foot in front of the other. DO NOT RUN.

The pretence of normality, as if passing the time of day, looking over the railings into the children's playground. Would this be easier if I was truly old? A time might come when people didn't turn their heads, I'd be invisible. But not yet. Not to the young girl staring at me from the playground, so entranced with the spectacle I made that she ignored the calls of a friend on the swings behind her.

A memory of childhood: perched in my tree (shimmering copper leaves) in the back garden of our house in Hampstead. Invisible, as I thought, to anyone on the ground. Invisible certainly to the old woman in the garden next door. Just an old woman, except that perhaps she wasn't so old, perhaps no more than sixty, or less, in any case someone to be mildly curious about only because she was afflicted in some way, referred to by adults in hushed voices, as if to speak louder was to risk contagion. The woman, old or not, had two sticks to support her, and was somehow stuck, half turning back to the house, as if she'd thought better of a walk down the garden, but could neither go back nor proceed.

Now I caught sight of a wispy figure. The apparition seemed to dog my steps. Several times now I had seen him standing in the same place on the corner of the square. Most people stared at me with curiosity—with amusement if they thought I was drunk, with fear if they were older and thought they recognised their own fate in mine. But he looked with a keen, objective interest, his eye following my progress round the square. I'd turned him into a beneficent figure, in preference to the dread I initially associated with his appearances. No longer afraid of him, I concentrated on walking forward in stately fashion, hoping he'd register my smooth progress, my wily control.

The girl still stared. Should I smile? Smile. But no, the child turned away, ran off to join her friend. And I was on my toes again, clutching, until I thought to relax my grip, just a fingertip would do it.

Still, I kept falling. My injuries were like those sustained in a school playground—chipped front tooth, grazed knee, sprained ankle—but with the additional old-age risk of a broken hip, so I began to take tablets. It was some weeks before they had an effect, but when it happened it was dramatic. I was walking with Victor on the Heath, with my usual tendency to rush forward uncontrollably, my sailor's lurch, when suddenly, from one moment to the next, from one footstep to the next, my stride lengthened, smoothed out, and I found my pace again. Victor, noticing it too, commented, and I replied, "Don't say anything," as if my reprieve might not hold if we paid it too much attention. It lasted three hours, and then just as suddenly I lost it, but only until the next tablet kicked in. For a time I was saved.

But then I began to be erratic in company, prone to making aggressive statements that offended people. It seemed to me that I always had a good reason for my rudeness, which usually came out of my irritation at someone's complacency. Victor said that at the best of times I was more than usually vehement, that these lightning switches of mood in me shocked people including him. It seemed to me I was simply stating an opinion, and as far as I was concerned this was an advance on my previous inability to say anything at all unless it was to ask simple questions about someone's métier or marital status. According to Victor it was alright to be vehement about some things, things that mattered, but not about little things like the shape of a car or the colour of a wall. For me, then, everything seemed to matter. But the vehemence didn't insult people as my lapses into aggression did. These remarks were completely unexpected, they seemed to come out of some previously hidden recess of my mind, taking me by surprise as much as they did my targets. Immediately I had spoken I regretted it and would apologise and then follow up with a remorseful card. But a little later I'd feel the essential truthfulness of what I had said, if not the absolute truthfulness, then my continuing belief in the veracity of my statement, even if I still felt shame for saying it. I wondered at how, once, I had been able to coast along amicably enough with these truths about people in my head, but still I regretted speaking them because it did no good and changed nothing, especially not for me.

I had crossed a border I could never traverse again, between health and sickness, autonomy and dependence, life and death. A response had to be made. I couldn't go on as I had before; rather, as I saw it, a fundamental change in my way of life was called for. Ever again, once and for all—these were phrases often in my mind then, as if conclusiveness could be achieved, was even desirable. I felt trapped, trapped by an illness that would soon make me dependent, trapped by the man I was dependent on, trapped not least by my lack of means. I found myself imagining ways I might suddenly get a lot of money. Someone would leave me a house which I'd sell for an enormous sum—this despite the fact that I knew no one with a valuable house who might leave it to me. I imagined being kind to some shabby, lonely old man who would gratefully leave me the fortune he kept under his mattress. Then I thought of doing the lottery with a series of numbers made up of my birth date and Victor's, and though I never placed a bet, every week I'd check to see if the numbers came up.

A friend spoke of friends of his who'd bought a house by the sea in Denmark. It cost them almost nothing, this house: there was a story about a farmer's wife, or widow, who owned the house—it was on land belonging to the farm—and whose children didn't want to become farmers. And so when these friends of our friend saw the empty house, raised above the dunes, overlooking a wide empty beach and the sea, and went to the farmer's wife and asked to buy it, she agreed. Apparently there were lots of such houses because people in Denmark preferred to live in the city or leave their country altogether. The story set me thinking. The idea of a house by the sea in Denmark—a place I'd barely ever thought of before—seemed irresistible. I imagined a wooden shack with a veranda along the front, and sitting on the veranda to watch the sun sink into the sea and, once the sun had gone and there was a chill in the air, sitting inside the shack beside an old-fashioned stove and listening to the waves breaking on the shore.

I went to the library and took out some guidebooks, and then I found out about flights to Copenhagen, and tried to make contact with the friends of our friend to learn more details. I was all set to go. Finally I got hold of them, and it turned out that our friend had got the story wrong. The house didn't overlook the sea, it was several miles inland. And it wasn't in Denmark but in Sweden—it was just that you could get to it from Denmark, crossing the causeway from one country to the other. Also, though the house was very cheap it needed many repairs, which they, being handy people, were doing themselves. As far as they knew there weren't lots of such houses, and finding theirs had been chance. All in all I had to let it go.

I asked myself what I would do if I was alone in the world, for one reason or another. Obviously I'd have to change everything. I'd have to move to a distant suburb, or another town, or the countryside. And then, though I'd have little choice but to go on with the work I did now, I would live simply. I wouldn't eat meat or drink wine, go to cafés, travel, see films, or ever spend recklessly in a shop. I'd stay at home, living modestly on the pittance I earned, with my cats for company, and reading books borrowed from the library. This, too, was a fantasy and, with its stringent, heroic aspect, by no means an unbearable one.

I also asked myself how it was that I did work that didn't guarantee my way of life, and it seemed impossible, because too late, to do any other kind of work. But then I thought that I must have had a hunch which had led me to make the choices I had, mainly the choice to write, and that if I were faithful to that hunch and waited long enough, it would bear fruit or at least a ray of light would fall on my situation and then I would understand it and know what to do and perhaps even have the power to do it. I kept thinking of that ray of light, about what it meant, which was partly elucidation. But perhaps it was also the spotlight into which I would walk to collect my unearned prize. It was my lucky moment.

It came, my ray of light, one early morning with a call from my godfather Lomas. When I'd said goodbye to him, I went to tell Victor what was proposed. He was in the bath, rinsing shampoo out of his hair. I sat on the lavatory lid and waited till he'd finished.

"That was Lomas."

"Oh?"

"He's offering us the Orkney house for the winter."

41

"What do you mean?"

"What I say. He wants someone there because last winter it became infested with rats. He's away for three months, from January to March. Long enough for us to settle in and get some work done, with nothing to distract us."

Victor hoisted himself out of the bath and when he quickly grabbed a towel to hide his nakedness I knew he was upset with me. He was unyielding: "It's out of the question," he said before I'd even finished my explanation. "I'm committed to things here. Anyway, how would we live?"

"I'll go on editing as I do here. Publishers post work out, and it doesn't make any difference whether they send it to the next street or to the other end of the country."

"Well, you've obviously made up your mind."

He left the bathroom, and I followed him. "I haven't made up my mind. I hoped we could discuss it."

"I can't go. It's very simple. If you want to, then you'd better do it, though it'll be the first time we've gone our separate ways."

"No, it won't. What about America—you were away for two months."

"I see, this is a revenge, is it?" He was pulling shirts out of a drawer as if he couldn't find the one he wanted. I stood at the door of the bedroom, afraid of his anger, and of my own resolution.

"Of course it's not. The circumstances are completely different."

"Why bring it up then?"

"Because you said—oh come on, I was questioning your histrionic suggestion that I'm walking out on you."

"Well, aren't you?"

"I want you to come too."

"So you've decided to go, come what may. This is hardly a discussion."

"You're just turning the tables on me, misrepresenting everything I say." He was pulling a shirt over his head, and his next words were muffled. "… what you have to do."

"What?"

"You must do what you have to do. But know that I can't join you."

"Well then, I won't go." And I left the room.

Later, he came to find me at my desk. He stood behind me and I didn't turn round.

"Look, I can't go. I can't and I don't want to. And I won't pretend I'm happy about your going alone. Can you cope on your own? But you must do what you want—always."

I became ill, ordinarily ill, like anyone might, with flu. I lay on the bed and stared out of the window at a brick wall. I picked up the book at my side and read a few lines wherever it fell open. Or closed my eyes in hope of sleep—and daydreamed of the wondrous house I'd given Belle … I came to with a start. Victor was sitting at the end of the bed. He heard my description of Belle's rural paradise and proceeded to denounce nature and solitude as poison.

"We'd be mad," he said, "to flee our lives in London, to imagine we could sustain an existence in an alien countryside. I can't drive and you soon won't be able to—you have to have a car in the country. Nor are we handy. And you can't even encounter a cow without going into a blue funk. Anyway, Belle wanted only to get away from the country and get to Paris."

"It's not as simple as that. She wanted to get away from her husband."

"I see."

"But that's not what I want."

"No?"

"No."

43

"What do you want then? I suppose this is all a part of the adjustment to your illness. In a year's time you'll see it for what it is."

"Oh? What's that?"

"Flights of fancy." He jumped up and began to stride round the room. He stood at the window but not as if he was looking at anything, rather as if he was composing his next sentences in his head. Then he turned towards me and said between gritted teeth, "You've become so discontented. You never used to be like this. It's as if nothing can make you happy."

At a loss for words of explanation, I turned away from his own desperation, his sense of entrapment—did I even see them?—and burying my face in the pillow, sought oblivion in thoughts of Belle's escape.

BELLE'S GREAT ESCAPE

Neither moon nor stars lit the rolling hills around the house. Belle, sleepless, sat up and traced a faint looming where black sky met a blacker earth. An irrelevancy preoccupied her: that she hadn't recognised the signs. And this despite having imagined his infidelity so often, as if it would have released her from her own obligations. They had been calm in those months. She was busy with her writing and Charles rarely impinged on her thoughts. It had seemed to her, fleetingly one evening, that at last they'd found a way of coexisting peaceably.

Ruth, her friend and helper, found her in yesterday's clothes when she brought in the morning coffee—as if the nightly ritual of sleep had escaped her notice. When she drew her attention to her crumpled dress Belle seemed baffled. But she went meekly to the basin, stood passively while Ruth poured water, handed soap and towels, gently helped her get out of her clothes. And then, as if her will suddenly asserted itself, Belle went at the job of washing with immense, excessive zeal.

Perhaps it was Ruth who arranged her getaway, for Belle was incapable of it—and it was against her principles to leave a marriage. Unless Charles himself understood the necessity— her need to distance herself, his own to consider his position, the impossibility of continuing as they were—and set about making the arrangements. And paying for them, for he possessed what she had brought to the marriage and perhaps, in his chagrin, was more than ready to finance her escape. A ticket for the journey to Paris, somewhere for her to stay, money to live on. Belle didn't have to spell out the terms. Charles, that most practical of men, bought his way out of trouble.

Who knows who might have seen her?—seen and taken note, of a woman dressed in a pale-coloured costume, an eau de nil, not the most sensible of colours for travelling. A certain disarray marked her—the garment had once been stylish but had now lost its crisp line and hung a little baggily on her. It was as if for many weeks her looks had been the last thing on her mind. Her hair was harshly and thoughtlessly pulled back from her face which was blotched with red. Since she was of an age when women for the most part went unnoticed, perhaps her fellow travellers didn't see her agitation. Her lips moved in silent conversation with herself or some absent other, and her hands twisted a handkerchief for something to do. But then, it was as if she decided: enough, life goes on, mine no less than anyone else's—and with a determined air she opened her bag and took out a book, opened the book, and appeared to read.

In the days that followed, whenever the coach stopped she looked up. Her hand tightened its grasp on the book, anxiety tensed her forehead. Did she expect to be dragged off, prevented from reaching her destination? Only when the coach set off again did she sink back into the seat, and close her eyes for a moment before going back to her book. But then—on the last leg of the journey, when streets and houses replaced fields beyond the window—she peered out and held herself tightly as if to quell her excitement.

She struggled through the crowd towards the Rivettes—two smiling faces bobbing up between backs of heads only to disappear again. They greeted her with hugs. Paul took her case,

Agnes her arm. There was no call for her to speak since they answered their questions for her: What a crowd! Has her journey been a trial?—How pale she looks, and hungry, but they've made a lamb stew … a glass of wine; is she really to stay a year? They've found her an apartment, a steep climb up but lots of sky to make her feel at home; what's she reading?—she looked down at the book she still clutched in her hand and couldn't remember, but Paul lifted her arm and proclaimed "Pascal", to which Agnes, astonished, cried, "On a coach!"

Then, in the carriage, one on each side of her, they calmed down. Agnes was still holding her arm and Paul now gently took her hand. Faltering, her voice pitched high from strain, at last Belle managed to speak. "I—have—taken—a—great—step."

A long climb up past imposing doors, coming at last to one so small it might have been a cupboard. They all stood panting as Paul managed the key. Then the tentative entry into an eyrie—so high, so safe—and the flood of sunlight on that particular morning, streaming into every room like the light of heaven.

"We were worried about the view, that you can't see the street. We'd want to."

But she preferred not to know there was a street. Streets frightened her to begin with, she couldn't find her pace and people seemed to stare.

"It's very small—the rooms are small—but at least there are several."

And each one off a corridor. She liked the corridor, for walking up and down.

"You could work at the kitchen table. There's no one to disturb you."

She especially liked the kitchen, its big sky.

How many ways of describing a sky. How many different skies to describe. Usually from the point of view of a building, as if a sky needed a foil, as a landscape did.

47

A great copper dome in the distance that would catch an early morning sun, so dazzling she'd have to look away. Yes, in that wet spring she was able to describe to her friends a dawn sky that was transparent blue.

In a drizzle the dome would turn green against a low grey sky. When the sky turned bilious it hardly showed.

And not only the dome, but a church tower, and the river a silver slick to one side visible if she pressed her face against the window, and endless series of roofs, some with figures on them—a woman hanging up washing, a man tending his pigeons, children with a kite.

She turned away from the view and laughed. The anxious-looking faces of Paul and Agnes broadened into relieved smiles. It was decided.

Solitude—she wondered that she'd had to endure a marriage to achieve it. She wanted only to stay in her attic and walk from room to room, arrange her books, and stand at the window and look at the view.

Once she had settled, her greatest pleasure was to go into a café, sit down, order a coffee, and open a book. Opening the book was the point. Not reading it or drinking the coffee, but having ordered the coffee, opening the book in preparation for reading it once she'd drunk the coffee. What was it about this act? The freedom of reading—not that Charles wasn't a reader as she was, not that she hadn't always made her own rules. But to open a book in the midst of a crowd who took not the slightest notice of her and know that she might read undisturbed with only the deadline of the café's closing time—this was joy.

BENJAMIN: Charles would acquire a posthumous reputation in his ancestral village: was said to have fathered at least one child there. But it's often claimed that it was Belle's affair, with a younger man, that rocked their marriage, bringing about her removal to Paris. It seems unlikely from what we know of her principles; also the pattern of her relationships. What she was best at was passionate friendship conducted mostly by letter—what she had had with d'Hermenches would now, by an odd chance, be mirrored by his young nephew.

As Benjamin would describe their meeting, at a salon in Paris, as soon as he set eyes on her, he understood her significance for him. She stood apart, silently watching, with that look on her face he would come to know well, which was partly disdain but also an acute awareness. Then, when she spoke, she expressed herself with originality and liveliness, with a contempt for conventional opinion that was exactly what people noted—and criticised—in him.

For Belle, it was nothing like that. There was little in his appearance that could possibly draw her—wasn't one young man much like another? Only the fact of his being the nephew of d'Hermenches marked him out. And that he had read her novels, had something to say about them.

They talked, that first time, about freedom, mainly Benjamin's lack of it. His father, the most controlling of men, it seemed to Belle, demanded that his son return home to the job that had been set up for him—when nothing was so obnoxious to Benjamin as the feeling that his freedom and independence of movement were endangered.

"So, what do you want to do?" she asked.

"Go to England and roam about."

"Ah! An escapade, a vagabond's life in the land of the free. Excellent!"

Flight had been Belle's solution, and she was keen to encourage others to follow her example. Never mind that she would return to Charles, and that Benjamin would eventually fall in with his father's plans for him.

Meanwhile, they were rarely seen except together. They attended meetings, readings, parties, and they talked in transit, on their way from one event to the next. As they talked, they explored the city, and with each new street or building

49

discovered, one or other expressed yet another opinion that had them exclaiming at their affinity.

Others would see her steal a glance at her young friend, a look of intense, and private, excitement. Who knows what she hoped for? In any case it didn't really figure, since Benjamin sought only affirmation, and glowed in the warmth of her understanding.

As he saw it in those early weeks of friendship in Paris, she helped him find his gift: "I have given up the idea of a novel," he would write to her from England. "I am too talkative by nature. All those people wanting to speak for me. I like to speak for myself, above all so that you can hear me."

It's unlikely he misled her. He told her about a mad plan to marry for money so as to clear the debts that made him dependent on his father's goodwill. She looked askance, laughing harshly as if at a bad joke. And then said something about people who have no thoughts for anything but their own ups and downs—delivered with a searching glance that he shiftily evaded, launching into an account of what he planned to do in England.

It was Charles who paid for his passage across the Channel. A year after Belle's arrival in Paris, he had written to suggest he might join her, since he too felt stale and in need of the stimulus of a city for a time—as if it was understood between them that their separation was only a temporary expedient, and sooner or later she would return.

She found him at her door one afternoon, patiently waiting. She came along the street and saw a thin figure leaning against a tree and reading a newspaper. At first she took it to be Paul, and quickened her pace. But then, oddly, when she realised her mistake, rather than feeling disappointed, or even appalled, she was touched. He looked vulnerable, a countryman overwhelmed by the mayhem of the city, using his paper as a defence against the curious glances of passers-by. Clearly he had come to fetch her home.

Perhaps she had always known that her sense of loyalty would permit no other ending. Also, she admitted to feeling uneasy at the centre of things, preferring always a life on the margins. She was too outspoken, too impatient of etiquette to tolerate Parisian hypocrisies, which couldn't accommodate her uncompromising truthfulness.

Perhaps Benjamin made it possible—and necessary—for her to return. Their friendship would make it bearable—and the presence in her life of a tolerant husband would allow her complete freedom.

"You don't mind?" Belle feared he'd regard her request for Benjamin's fare as outrageous.

"Haven't I always accepted your friends? I'm glad to help a young man on his way, though I don't think his father will thank us for it."

"They'll have to be reconciled eventually."

"But for the time being an adventure will do the boy no harm."

Belle was perhaps too taken up with her young friend to see that Charles might have another motive. If he was jealous he didn't show it, but perhaps he saw how it was for her, and for her own sake as much as his own wanted Benjamin's removal.

... AND MINE

I descended into a house that was not, as I had feared, dark and chill, for Victor had stoked the stove before leaving and switched on the table lights so that eddies of warmth greeted me. I felt the loss of him keenly, as a dull ache in my side, and wondered at his goodness in bringing me to that place.

I sat at the kitchen table with a cup of tea. Slowly the dim light of morning gave form to what lay outside: the field in front of the house, the road, the lake beyond, and finally the sea, a strip of dark grey beneath a low, bruised sky. I watched the sheep in the field, and some swans flying over the lake, and a bus rounding the lake to stop at a farm on the far side. Suddenly, my view was blocked by a creature on the window-sill, my companion, the cat Iso. I got up and opened the window, which the wind almost wrenched out of my hand, and Iso came in, yowling for food.

In several more layers of clothes, I took the track down to the sea, and the wind came at me, so that every step was an effort and I thought only of putting one foot in front of the other. When at last I reached the water I looked for the seals that had appeared for Victor, as he said they would for me, curious to watch and stare.

I called out, as he had done, doubting that my voice, cracked by self-consciousness, could reach the seals above the sounds of wind and water. But then they appeared, smooth black heads bobbing about on the waves, and sniffing the air as if they heard or saw with their snouts. I counted six of them before turning away to walk back to the house, the wind behind me now, carrying me along as if I was sailing.

Later, I set out for the shop. The road rose steeply upwards. Land, sea, air alike were spacious, but not the houses, which huddled here and there, low and ugly, into dips in the hill, as if seeking shelter from the hurtling gales. By the time I reached the crest of the hill I felt hot and unbuttoned my coat which then flew behind me, almost torn off my arms by the wind, so that I had to turn round and with my back to the wind do it up again. Then I took off my hat, but my loosened hair blew across my face and blinded me.

A crowd of people filled the shop. They gave no sign of noticing me until my turn came and then they stopped their talk to hear me declare myself. I asked for the items I wanted— "Not too many," I said, in the way of conversation, "so I can carry them."

"Where have you got to carry them to?"

"To Lomas's, I'm looking after Lomas's place. You must be Marie—Lomas mentioned you."

"How are you managing?"

"So far so good,"—and I laughed, too loudly, and when Marie echoed my laugh she also sounded false, and quickly asked: "Doesn't Lomas have a car?"

"It's broken down," I said, "and since it doesn't have a licence, as Lomas explained it, I thought I wouldn't bother with it, I'll walk, it's good for me."

"Aye," said Marie, "if you've got the strength."

And a woman standing near said, "Billy Kidd will fix it, and no one bothers with licences, do they?"—looking round at the company and someone laughed.

Marie said, "Aye, Billy Kidd," and gave me his number.

Walking back with the bags of groceries, which were almost more than I could carry though they would last me only a few days, I stopped at the phone box to ring this Billy Kidd. He heard me out and said he'd come over, but not that day, and if not the next then the one after.

I didn't like to leave the house in case he came. I kept an eye on the road because I couldn't hear anything above the soughing wind, not a car come up the track, nor a caller shouting, and though I thought Billy Kidd was likely just to walk in and keep on going until he found me, since what else could people do in the circumstances, I couldn't risk missing him.

He didn't come that day, or the next. And not till the afternoon of the day he'd set as his deadline did I dare stray further than the yard, and then walked up the hill behind the house where I could keep the road in sight. The sun showed itself for the first time since my arrival, and sky and sea became a blue so intense that it was like the south, and not the south I'd come from, but further still: Amalfi perhaps. Except for the sodden green land and the treelessness, and above all the wind so I stood long enough only to watch a boat make its way choppily across my view until it disappeared round a headland. But still no Billy Kidd.

He came at last when my back was turned, and got on with the job. I went out to feed the geese and found the barn door open and a man with his head under the bonnet of the car. "Shouldn't let it waste," he said in greeting, as if I was resisting the idea of driving the car.

He joined me after for a dram, and we talked of the stove. Every morning I woke to find it fading, and before anything else could be done it had to be brought back to life, and then every minute fussed over, my only source of warmth and hot water and cooked food.

"These days people have electric cookers and heaters. They may still have their stoves but not to depend on."

"Lomas hasn't got round to it yet," I said. "For years he's been only a summer visitor."

"Aye," said Billy Kidd, "ayee. Summers are easy, it's the winters you have to look out for."

I'd read about the Viking bands that had holed up there and drank themselves numb through days that were mostly nights. Nothing much had changed, it seemed. Winter consisted of waiting for spring as best you could.

Daily I walked down to the sea, either the nearby sea, the view from the house, where I sang to the seals; or the sea beyond the headland, where I stood on slabs of slate jutting out over heaving planes of water and looked towards even more northerly places—Iceland, or Norway. I watched it sucked into steaming eddies between the rocks, and then pulled back into the depths, a clatter of stones in pursuit. From a distance it sounded like a train, and there, at the edge, the roar deafened. Far out, in the curve of infinity, silence beckoned.

I seemed always to be watching, looking at what lay before me, and was blind when I tried to look inwards. I did the editorial work that was my living, but when I turned to Belle—to Benjamin's first, ecstatic visit to her at home—my concentration failed me. Instead, I tried writing of the view from the windows, but other people's words came out, as if it was impossible to write of landscape except in the words of literature, which were words of exalted feeling, of awe, when for me the landscape evoked unease even if sometimes, when the sun came out, and the colour, it could also astound me.

More often, as I stared out of the window, I was bored by what I saw, so that when a car crossed the scene it was immediately more interesting, for the car contained a person and I could think about who that person might be and where they were going and why.

I sought the familiarity of Lomas, in the signs of him about the place, which were partly in its bareness, the absence of much thought in its arrangements, for he hardly noticed his surroundings and gave no time to making a home, though there were odd touches of comfort, like the daybed by the fire, where he lay to read by an excellent lamp; and partly in objects, such as the shelf of treasures, mementoes of his years in Africa, each one specially chosen or received, a stone, a shell, a carved wooden deity; or the row of his shoes and boots by the back door, battered but clean, and dependable in their upright orderliness.

I lived a life of extreme regularity, dictated by the timing of the medication I took. In one sense the pills, having to remember to take them, exerted a tyranny that never allowed me to forget I was sick, but mainly, as tools of control, they liberated me. So long as I remembered to take them at exactly the right time, for much of the day I was fit and active—and if I forgot or they failed to kick in I just sat at home until they took effect. I was never required to be anywhere or to see anyone and could easily enough accommodate the fluctuations in my condition.

Standing at the sink one early morning as the kettle slowly filled, I looked out into the retreating darkness and listened to the radio news. It was the same news I would have heard in the south, spoken in a familiar voice, though I heard it in a place so far from home, so remote from anything I knew, that for a moment I didn't know where I was, I felt in both places, split, or in neither place. Then my mind went blank and I couldn't recall anything, as if the different bits of me had atomised, and all I was aware of was my hand on the tap, as if it clutched at stability while the rest of me threatened to disintegrate. And then the sodden green of the field emerged before me, and the milky lake, and the grey band of the sea separating from the low, swollen sky, and I saw too that the kettle had filled and water dripped down its sides, and Iso was on the window-sill, and the newly replenished stove crackled, and the newsreader spoke of traffic jams on a motorway into London, and then I came back together again and continued the motions of morning.

I visited an ancient burial place, a cairn protected by a large prefabricated shed: rows of tombs, each with its stone bunk where a corpse would have lain. A raised walkway traversed the length of the chamber, with creaking wooden slats and a metal handrail rusty and yet damp to the grasp. A musty-smelling place suggesting bats in its girdered heights and rats in its shadowed depths, but what undermined me was not only these associated horrors but the sense of enclosure, of entrapment, for the door had clicked shut behind me. Fear tightened its grip on me and all I could think of was getting out, or not being able to, and I started to run, the walkway shuddering with my heavy footfall. I jumped down the steps and tried to force the door, which at first wouldn't open because of my hamfistedness. When at last I got it open I fled.

I headed for the promontory, stumbling on tufts and clods and then on a heap of matted wool that was firm against my foot: a sheep, and dead.

I picked myself up and veered off inland as the day turned dark and troubled, clouds banking blackly over the brae. I ran against the wind which seemed to want to force me back towards the cairn and the dead sheep. But then my walking began to fail, and I was limping and then dragging my feet, and feeling drained and exhausted, but nonetheless got back to the house where I collapsed on to the couch in the living room.

I watched a hearse go by on the road: a long black hatchback. As it crossed my view it seemed to become a ghostly progression in the murky afternoon light. I watched it turn off the road and come up the track towards the house, and as it got closer it seemed first to get blacker and then to fade into the dingy surrounds, and when I went out to greet the driver I saw that it wasn't a hearse but an ordinary, featureless van, and not black but green. The driver was delivering something for Lomas, some shelves he'd ordered from a carpenter.

Later, when the man had gone, and I sat at the kitchen table with a purring Iso on my lap and drank tea, I asked myself why I had mistaken a van for a hearse. I decided it was partly the poor light, but that alone wasn't enough to explain my error. There was something else as well. It was as if an archetype of death had taken hold of me.

Things began to break and fail. First, a piece fell off the stove, a brick positioned just inside the door, which broke up as it fell inwards into the flames. I worried that it mattered, that brick, and such little worries began to fill my life, taking the place of big worries, though they threatened, these little worries, to coalesce into a larger one.

Snow came, a scattering of powder, striping the brown-green hills with white. I found on Lomas's shelves a volume of tales of the old Icelanders who, six centuries before me, listened to the telling of what I in my solitude read in a book. It occurred to me that, just like the islanders, these stories ignored the landscape and the weather. The remarkable day, for them, was the day when the wind didn't blow too much, and there wasn't ice or snow or mud, and no one got cold or wet, which happened rarely, and so the landscape and the elements were just a backcloth to be forgotten, when for me they ruled everything and once I had taken them into account there was no escaping them.

When water ceased to flow from the taps, Marie at the shop said it was an island problem, the silting up of water pipes, and that a compressor would fix it. The people to go to for a compressor were the Robertsons at the farm across the lake: Alan—who appeared when I knocked, looked bleary-eyed at me, and stumbling turned away—and Shona—who came in his place, looked askance as she heard my story, and didn't ask me in out of the wind and rain. She agreed, though, to lend the machine.

First, clumsily, I unscrewed the pipe to the mains at the back of the house, as Shona had described it, but then couldn't fix the compressor to the pipe, and even if I had been able to, I feared turning on the electrics that would galvanise it, because if it worked the water would gush out and perhaps I'd not be able to stop it, by screwing up the pipes again, and the puddle at my feet would fast become a lake, what with the rain and the rivulets too that splashed down the hillside.

Meanwhile a trickle of water found its way past the scarf round my neck and I felt the icy trail down my back. I cursed the Robertsons, and I cursed Lomas, and even Victor, and then I cursed myself for the hubris that had deluded me into believing I could survive in such a place, let alone handle a compressor. And then, finally, I went in to call Marie, not knowing who else to turn to, and heard the catch in my voice, the threatening tears, which Marie would hear too, and sent her husband, who'd just come in and still wore his outdoor clothes.

So Marie's Tony fixed it and accepted my jabbering thanks, but wouldn't come in for a dram, being so wet, and then it was as if the worst had happened and I had lived to tell the tale, which was how I put it in a letter to Victor, composed in my head as I lay in a hot bath and thought how I'd open some wine. Later the cat Iso got into the mood of things and after gobbling my dinner scraps sat on the kitchen table and gazed at me as I thought of what I had left behind in London, of Victor, whom I'd so recklessly abandoned, our flat, and life together, and then of what had brought me there, the restlessness that came with the illness, the impossibility of going on as before. It never occurred to me that I might not return, nor did I doubt that Victor would have me, but still I carried with me a sense of distance between us. The unquestioning love and admiration that I had felt for him, and believed he had felt for me, had been undermined by our responses to my illness. I had been dismayed by his failure, as I saw it, to understand my needs; and he, no less so, by my sudden dependency, and its frightening implications for his future, which my demands seemed to encapsulate. And though the crack might be repaired, had to some extent been so by his accompanying me to the island, it had happened and I feared would leave its permanent scar of distrust. But then I imagined Victor visiting me, so that it seemed for a while, in my cups, as if I was waiting for the letter that would announce his arrival and even for his arrival itself.

I wrote to him regularly, short notes that spoke straightforwardly of my days. He sent me cards, with similarly conventional messages—but I knew that for Victor it was all in the image and to this I always paid attention.

About half way through my stay, he sent a picture of a sculpture by Brancusi: a block of stone carved with two pairs of embracing arms, and four eyes, and two mouths squashed sideways because their faces were pressed so tightly together. Hair—undulating lines—flowed down the back of the woman and was cropped on the scalp of the man.

This was followed, a couple of weeks later by an Egyptian pair statue—a husband and wife standing side by side, her arm tight round his waist, and his round her neck, a hand flat on her breast, strong and upright like comrades.

To break my isolation I attended a musical evening at a bar on the other side of the island. It was no more than half full when I arrived, and not seeing a place at one of the tables where people already sat, and in any case worrying that it might seem presumptuous to sit with people I didn't know, I took a place at an empty table, where no one else sat down until all the other seats were taken, and the last guests, who turned out to be Shona and Alan Robertson, had no alternative but to join me.

Her mother, who accompanied them, carried the day. The old woman was deaf like so many people on the island, presumably because of the wind, and couldn't hear a single word that was said to her. That didn't stop her talking a great deal herself which, in view of her son's moroseness and Shona's and my effortfulness, was to be welcomed. Alan broke his silence only once, to ask, quite out of the blue, if I knew what an FEB was. "Fucking English Bastard," he said, and threw back his head with a mad, braying laugh. And so it was until the fiddle started up and we three women sat back to listen while Alan stolidly drank his way though many drams.

A man called John, who Marie put me on to when the barn door blew in one night in a gale, and who came every day for a week to mend it—John told me many things. He spoke of the quarrels between island families, who carried their feuds from one generation to the next, that Marie and Tony for example were at the throats of the family that owned the bar, and that their feud, whose origins lay deep in the past, now played itself out on the local council. He said that Alan Robertson was sometimes found drunk in a ditch, and this was Shona's cross which she bore resentfully. And he explained that there were two ways to live on the island, and one was to get involved, and the other was not to, but that if you were an incomer you were judged meddling if you chose the first, and snooty if the second. So while he, John, as an islander, could be remote, a bit of a recluse, which he was, I as an incomer could not be—not that anyone would like me more for not being, and not that it applied in my case anyway because I was just a visitor and people thought of me, if they thought of me at all, as a tourist.

At last the day came when I walked out and was able to unbutton my coat without the wind's wrenching it off me. The first spring day, and I walked over the hill at the back of the house to the ruins of an old church. I poked about the graves and read the inscriptions and imagined those dead men and women, especially the young ones. It was as if, I thought, I was burying something—grief for my illness, perhaps, and all its attendant distortions, even the disease itself—and I felt taken out of myself, almost in ecstasy, or delusion, which came from the blueness of the sea all around and the greenness of the turf and the playfulness of the birds and the softness of the air, and it was as if everything that had happened to me had been leading up to this moment, which was the point of it all—and this feeling stayed with me after I had returned to the house and with Iso watched from the window as night fell.

When the car failed, finally, I didn't phone Billy Kidd but decided to rely on my own two feet. At the shop Marie was all concern but saw the sense of it—put it away and forget about it, one less worry. That day Marie's Tony was driving my way and gave me a lift with the shopping; another, Shona Robertson passed near the crest of the hill and stopped to pick me up. Now that my time was almost over it was as if she remembered herself, put herself out, and agreed to come in for tea. She sat at the kitchen table and told of her son in Australia, so that I felt her poignancy, her sense of being stranded on the island, and her longing for her grandchildren; and her silence about her husband was more moving than complaints, of which she must have had many.

As she got up to leave she thought to ask whether I had been lonely on the island so far from home, and I said that yes, I had, but that was what I had come for, to be lonely, to see where it got me, and Shona replied that she could understand that, that loneliness wasn't the worst thing so long as you were on your own, though if you weren't it might be. And went on her way as if it was something to have said it.

As my departure approached, my imagination, ahead of me, let go of the place: it no longer assaulted me and confined me in the present, but left my mind free to roam. I thought about how it would be to walk unimpeded by mud and wind and layers of clothes, in fact not to have to walk at all but to catch a bus to go somewhere. And to see faces that were pale rather than raw-red, and sharp and tense rather than round and open. And to enter a shop without turning heads and to give as good as I got.

I thought about Belle, the writing I might have done on the island, but hadn't, the writing I planned to do now.

Above all, I thought of Victor—and my only backward glance was at Iso, who seemed to sense I was leaving and disappeared on the morning of my last day as if to save us both from the sadness of parting.

THE PINK HOUSE

Benjamin had written that he would walk from the coach stop, but now it occurred to Belle that he might ignore her precise directions and cut across the fields to the house. She turned at the thought, stumbling slightly in her haste, as if she expected him to appear from the opposite direction, stealing up on her from behind to take her by surprise.

Confused, she considered the awkwardness of her position, waiting for the speck on the road that would announce him and rushing down the hill like an eager young lover (she blushed). Probably she'd fall, or twist her ankle, and in any case present the most ungainly sight, a woman with the thick figure of middle age, cantering down the track, landing at his feet out of breath (since she spent most of her life at a desk) so that she couldn't greet him but only puff in his face. Or she could wait where she was, subjecting him to the embarrassment of being watched as he climbed the hill.

She looked down at the house—a particular view that had been her first sight of it when she returned. She'd come over the brow of the hill and seen it and something in her had responded, a moment of recognition. Oh, these guarded acceptances. Why couldn't she acknowledge that as a matter of fact she loved the house?—that in her first sighting of it in the evening shadows she forgot her sense of resignation and actually felt her heart leap.

Not that the house had been part of her calculation, so far as she knew. She had rarely thought of it in the year and a half of her absence. She certainly hadn't missed it, nor had it figured in her decision to return. It was Benjamin, their intimacy and its limits, that had made it both possible and necessary for her to return. But now, as she took in the trails of smoke along the valley, the bare branches of the huge old tree behind the house, the glimmer of water beyond the wood, she believed she was right to come back, or rather, since she had no choice but to come, that in the place itself she might find fulfilment.

She was about to walk back to the house to await him more conventionally (and the cold was taking hold of her) when he appeared, not as a speck on the horizon but already halfway up the hill and calling her name.

She ran towards him, slithering on the slippery surface of the road, but without falling. Laughing, they met, and he took her hands and swung her round and round until she begged him to stop.

Then he began to talk, gabbling some story about his journey she couldn't get the point of, and then about his father—always his father—which she listened to, as she had before, gently inclining her head as if to follow his words with the utmost attention, ready to give him the benefit of the doubt.

"A pink house!"—for some reason this was a surprise to Benjamin. She led him to her room at the back of the house, and for a moment he was shy, as if the intimacy of the room, with the desk, and her books and papers, made him aware for the first time in their short friendship that she had her own life, a writer's life and a wife's, and that though he had spoken of everything to her, she had been more cautious. "They all blame you for my flight," he told her.

65

"Ah, the malicious influence of a woman old enough to be your mother."

"That's it. Poor creature, motherless from birth and now the plaything of an authoress."

When Ruth came to remove the tea things she tightened her mouth so as not to laugh—at the visitor, the tall, skinny, red-haired young man who was charging back and forth, and Belle, who had that look of triumph on her face as when she'd outsmarted, without their realising it, one of the dullard neighbours. But Benjamin was equal to her cutting wit, they egged each other on—Ruth could see that at a glance as she backed out of the door with the tray. Rarely had she known Belle so animated, her cool eyes aflame.

At dinner they calmed down (no one could have kept it up in front of stolid Charles). The men behaved faultlessly to each other. Charles was responsive by his usual standards to Benjamin's literary overtures and their guest was unusually respectful of his host's remarks which he must surely—it seemed obvious to Belle—find mundane. She almost relaxed, but then Charles lost his way in an account of local politics, and she—she couldn't stop herself—snubbed him. Benjamin looked studiously away—from floundering Charles and defiant Belle—and then, to fill the silence, told a story about the dog that had been his companion in England.

Benjamin, the great talker, recorded one enduring memory of that visit to Belle. She writes at her desk, he stretches out on the couch reading. A memory of silence apart from the scratch of her pen, the turning of his pages, a memory of words but not spoken. A comfort for him, who had never before known the companionship of a like mind, let alone a home where nothing was required of him but to be himself.

ELLENORE: She lay wrapped in blankets over her day clothes because a nightdress made her feel exposed and defenceless. She traced the willow pattern of the torn wallpaper, the flood

66

cracks in the ceiling, and a bare branch which was all she could see out of the window. Sometimes she picked up one of the books that Adolphe had placed at her side. Or closed her eyes in hope of sleep. When she knew he was out, she got off the bed and shuffled through the house to the kitchen to make a hot drink for her swollen, aching throat.

Every so often he would appear and sit at the end of the bed and tell her how desperately he wanted to leave her. He said he felt guilty about her husband, and about his father who judged him, and fearful for his job. He said that their love was doomed because it could only flourish in isolation, opposed to the world they had known until then, and such an opposition, and such a love, were untenable. They must have been mad, he said, to flee their lives, to imagine they could sustain an existence in an alien countryside. He blamed himself more than he blamed her, but while he knew he should leave her, for his sake and hers, he was incapable of doing so.

He came in windswept from long walks through the winter landscape, but he never spoke of what he saw on those walks, of whom he met. He never described the farm where he bought their meagre supplies, or the inn where he picked up his mail, letters sent in reply to his desperate messages—to his employers, his father, and, for all she knew, her husband.

Endlessly he rehearsed their affair. Certain phrases haunted him—*folie d'amour, l'instant fatal, un poids énorme*—as if he was locked in the moment when, shocked and exhausted and breathless from their flight, they had arrived at the house and she had collapsed in a fever, and all he could think of was what madness had brought them there.

And perhaps because her fever made her slow it was many days before she could write some words on a scrap of paper. Next time he came to her she handed it to him. "What strange pity makes you afraid to break a tie which has become such a burden to you?" He stared at it wide-eyed before writing his reply, as if he too at last was speechless: "Why don't you leave me?"

Again it was several days before she could write her answer: "I would have left you if I'd had the strength."

And so the days, weeks even, passed. She continued to be ill and unable to speak, but as she lay there, her throat throbbing, and he said what he'd already said many times, a phrase came into her head and repeated itself: Must I die? Must I die? Must I die? And it occurred to her that there was only one possible end to his version of their story, and that end could only be her end—she must be written off. She would have liked to protest, to reach for pen and paper and write her dissent, but something in his voice, something so apparently rational, so beguiling and insistent, stopped her. And then she found she had moved her lips, whispering it—must I die? And perhaps because it was the first time she had spoken, he noticed, and asked her to say it again, and so, making a great effort, she croaked—*faut-il que je meure?* He stared at her and paled, and grinned crookedly to mask his shame—and from that moment on she began to recover.

ON-AND-ON-NESS

Victor's snores wake me, but not irrevocably. I sink back into sleep, and follow him into a wood. It feels forbidden, so we walk carefully, delicately, over mushy wet leaves. We come almost at once to a glade of brownish reddish mulch. At first I see nothing unusual, only a slight bulging of the leaves, so that the eye is drawn to and slowly, very slowly, makes out what remains of a human being. Except that nothing remains, it's a carcass, stripped now of anything an animal might find edible, reduced to gristly skin and bones amidst the mulch. Then I see that there's another—this one all ghastly vacant eye sockets beneath a frizz of white hair. Its trunk seems to peter out where its stomach might have been, except for a femur that lies in the leaves. I get no more than a glimpse, because Victor turns back to me and takes my hand to lead me, or to be led, away.

"No one has found them yet," he says.

"We have," I object.

"And now someone else will too. It happens like that."

I wake with a sense of inevitability, a calm understanding that the bodies are Victor's and mine, and that is to be expected, but then I fall into a troubled half-sleep. Now I'm trying to put great blocks of text into order. It's almost tangible, this attempt, this effort, as if it isn't just in my head, thinking, but

69

I'm actually lifting and pushing and shoving, and the blocks are slabs of concrete. I get them into order and then realise I've left one out, and I can't identify which one it is, so I start again with the ordering, and then before I reach the end I forget how it started and have to begin all over again. All I want is to sleep and forget the task, but I can't. So I get up.

If I give my brain a task to distract it, sometimes I can sneakily do what it doesn't want me to. So I stretch out the left hand as if to switch on the bedside lamp but don't—so as not to wake Victor. Then, while my brain thinks about what the left hand is up to, I coax the right foot up the bed so that the knee rises, and with the right hand grasp it and haul. It works if the foot stays flat on the bed, but tonight it won't, when I pull on my knee it jerks up towards my forehead and before I know it I'm on my back again. Fuck it! Anger can occasionally fuel the will. Roll the body over to one side, hoisting instead of hauling, left elbow taking the full weight as legs are inched over the side of the bed. A moment's pain as the weight shifts to the lower back, but almost at once I'm upright. Sitting, breathless with the effort of it, in pitch-black darkness—my feet are flat on the floor and I'm triumphant.

Victor is still snoring but not as evenly as before, and I wait till the snorts regain a rhythm before sliding to the edge of the bed. I let my head drop forward, and complete the momentum that takes me off the bed and on to my feet. Hurrah! I breathe deeply.

Next: the shuffle to the door, trying to remember the obstacles, shoes pulled off and dumped, clothes lying where they were dropped, a chair, not to mention the creaky board by the door, and being sure to step sideways, crab-style, over the threshold, so it doesn't freeze me. Along the corridor to the kitchen, feeling my way towards the sink where I switch on a tiny lamp, giving just enough light to see to make tea.

I stand dozily, waiting for the kettle to boil, one hip balancing me against the sink. Something outside catches my attention, breaks in. A sudden flicker through the trees in the square, as if someone has lit a cigarette. I imagine a deep draw, a pleasure long postponed, and the almost instantaneous kickback of guilt: whoever it is at once throws the cigarette to the ground and steps on it, since after that momentary flicker I see nothing more. I stare at the spot and seem to make out a black streak of a shadow which moves as if about to form into a figure, but then doesn't materialise. My apparition. I came to think of him as the ghost of Dr Parkinson who, two hundred years ago, walked in the streets just south of mine and observed persons he saw to be afflicted with the disease he defined. His essay hardly touches me now. It's as if I've developed a way of comprehending his account while somehow not applying it to my own case, as if a layer of cotton wool protects my raw nerves from the full imaginative impact of his words.

His appearances became so fleeting that I sometimes wondered if he existed at all other than as an apparently materialising shadow, a hallucination. Perhaps he was one of the solitary walkers, those who feel most themselves walking the streets. They might be seen anywhere, at any hour, in all weathers. They live to walk, and it's as if their survival depends on it, not only to dull some long-suffered pain of existence with the routine of physical exertion, but because, by the implicit offering of their goodwill to everyone they pass, they bestow grace on them, and find their own justification. Most people are blind to them, these guardian angels, but a few who are aware beyond their own concerns will notice the reappearance of the same walker again and again, as if he—or she—is tracking them. As the years pass they come to look out for him, even to acknowledge him. They see him age and slow, and then they see him rarely and then not at all, but it might be months before they note his absence and feel sorrow at his passing.

I focus again on the place in the trees, but nothing moves now; if he was there, he's gone.

I make a slow progression along the corridor to the room that's Victor's studio, bearing the cup of tea as if in an egg and spoon race. Victor, mildly regretful of the stains on the carpet, has suggested a tray, which is one thing too many to consider, so I move carefully, inching forwards, not to let my feet run away with me. I pull open the door, and slow to a creep in case I freeze to the spot, which can happen at any kind of threshold, as if I've come up against a brick wall. Stopping and starting, the clash of opposing forces, an implosion, from frozen in my tracks to an agitated run forwards—so that if I stop I can't start again, and once started, I can't stop.

Reaching the couch I place the tea on the table. Then I turn too abruptly so my feet stick and I start to topple, but I'm close enough to the couch to fall on it. I close my eyes. The sense of homecoming is so intense that a sob catches my breath.

Once, I railed against my short nights, but I've come to see that they suit me, and now I depend for my wellbeing on the two or three hours of quiet contemplation my insomnia allows me. I've even stopped thinking of it as insomnia. It's a time of clarity, the drug-free hours.

Victor has given me a corner of his studio to use in the night. Behind a screen is a couch with a small table beside it. Every evening I prepare the couch so that I can slip quickly under the blanket and, sipping a cup of tea, consider the books and papers on the little round table at my side. I'm cocooned by the light from a lamp on the floor behind me, and the room beyond the screen with its chaos of canvasses, piles of drawings, the plastic carrier bags in which Victor keeps his papers, the many images tacked to the walls, is lost in velvety blackness. Just as the world beyond is lost in silence. Only the smell penetrates to my corner, the heady, nose-tingling fumes of turpentine that overwhelm the gentler taste of tea. And then, my cup empty, I read, or, sometimes, write. If it is writing. Moving paragraphs around on a computer on my lap, stiffly, haltingly tapping out words that mostly I then discard—is this writing?

I've still things to write about Belle, my companion in the early years of Parkinson's, but I keep putting off the moment when I might finish. It's partly the business of the house. I came across an etching of the house Belle lived in with Charles, a large house made pretentious by its gracelessness, an ugly house in what looks like the scrappy outskirts of a town. I was oddly distressed by this discovery. I had posited my Belle on the idea of a house of heart-stopping beauty, a wonder, on the edge of a village deep in the countryside and now that I'm faced with the reality I fear for the integrity of my view of her.

But it's not only that. I've put it off also because to write The End would be to invite my own. Now it may be too late, this malady has dried up my juices; and when I look at these fragments of writing I see a mind that is stuck. This stuckness has become the chief attribute of my condition, in various manifestations. My fingers stick on the keyboard. My feet stick to the floor. My mind sticks in a groove, as if the range of possible associated thoughts is narrowing. I or my brain can't stray from a few well-trodden paths, and digs an ever deepening and engulfing furrow, a pit of obsession. What's to be done? I can't stop it, but perhaps I can make something of it. Put it to use. Turn it to gold.

A figure looms out of the darkness beyond the screen. Victor stands there in his pyjamas.

"So I woke you?"

He yawns in answer.

"You were asleep when I left."

"Only pretending to be."

"That was a very convincing snore."

"So it was me who woke us?"

"Who knows? I don't expect so."

"Are you working? You shouldn't work. You should lie quietly, concentrate on the pineal eye."

"I'm lying here quietly, minding my own business."

"Can I join you?"

I would rather he doesn't, knowing how it's likely to end, with his snoring beside me on the too small daybed, so I have to go back to the bedroom.

"You're too cavalier about this sleeplessness, it's bad for you." He climbs in beside me and we lie quietly for a while.

Anna just came for a visit. We took her on a walk along the south bank. She was full of little attentions, well-meant undoubtedly, but unwelcome to me, since I was fully drugged, as was surely evident, and didn't need Anna to fetch and carry for me. She was kind, she was thoughtful—but not so kind and thoughtful as to perceive what was really required.

I was already irritated when we got out of the lift at the top of the Oxo tower and I had an attack of vertigo. Not only did I feel in danger of throwing myself over the railing, but I feared for Victor and Anna too, and urged them back from the edge. But later, on a terrace at the Tate, I wasn't affected, which Victor said was peculiar, and Anna thought so too, as if I was guilty of inconsistency, as if they knew nothing about vertigo, how it took one differently at different times, and according to subtle differences in the location. (The vantage point at the Oxo tower juts outwards while the terrace at the Tate is enclosed on three sides.) I suggested that they carry on together while I returned to Anna's car and waited. Anna disagreed: we should carry on together, and if I got tired she would go and fetch the car; but Victor, who had had enough, wanted us all to go back to the car. So Anna said that I, as the invalid I suppose, should decide, and they would do what I wanted. But when I again voiced my preference, she insisted on her own plan.

It's always a struggle, and a temptation: to make illness my role, my identifying characteristic, rather than just another fact of life, however I might internalise it. I could have controlled my highly strung if not hysterical reaction to the drop from the Oxo tower, I didn't have to impose my vertigo on the others. And Victor was right when he said it was all a comedy, and the only thing to do was to laugh.

I laugh, and Victor beside me stirs. "What's funny?"

"I'm thinking about yesterday, Anna and all that."

"I'm glad you can laugh."

"It was silly. But she's too much. Perhaps I am too."

"Anna's Anna. We know how she is by now. And you— well, we know you too."

Yes, a woman who's become cranky, with her ticks and manias. A woman who's indefinably odd: with a slight unsteadiness and stiffness, a smile that has to be forced, a faint voice with blurry articulation, and in general a manner that jars when frailty breaks through a surface normality.

I wonder if Victor is nodding off until I feel his hand finding a way in under my sweater and then undoing the buttons of my nightdress, finding my breasts. I need the drugs for this; the drugs that stop me writing in the day time, dry up those juices, allow these ones to flow. Still, I seek his penis, which is stiff against my side, and fumble because my hand is clumsy, but though I can't work my best magic, I run one finger, as gentle as gossamer, deep into the central place he likes it best, and stroke him too from behind, my head on his chest, and soon he comes with a groan. But then, as he sighs happily and stretches out, he rolls with a little shout off the side of the daybed, and we both begin to laugh. He hoists himself back, and still laughing I make room for him, and we settle down in a squashed heap. Soon he begins to snore, but gently, little more than a whispering sigh that will surely lull me into sleep.

I picture Belle towards the end of her life, sitting at her desk, with her back to the window, not to be distracted by the view up the valley, reserved for naps on the daybed. Not long ago I came across a passage in a letter that I must have missed or was blind to in previous readings: "I never came back to the place without a sense of despair. I determined then never to leave it. And I have rendered it endurable." I count the years: eighteen. Shut away with Charles and his sisters, in a house that had become a prison, and all the more confining because her life sentence was self-imposed.

I see her form as if from the garden: upswept hair on her bowed head so her neck is revealed above a voile collar. A woman of excellence and distinction, who has committed herself to her work and will whatever the restraints on her freedom remain loyal to it till the end.

But something is hindering her, and it's more than fits of sleep. Her quarrel with Benjamin perhaps: he accused her of being squeamish about the revolution, insisting that you were either for the people or against them, and it was no good wanting change and balking at the consequences. He told her too, when she objected to his taking up with the Necker woman, that she, Belle, was smothering him. She had always been tolerant of his mistresses, even made a pet of his wife, so long as she (Belle again) remained his intellectual mainstay. Now Necker had stolen her role, or Benjamin had conferred it on her. Belle, who could ill afford to lose him, made it the breaking point, and pride dictated that the rupture come from her: "I like neither your way of life nor your friends, neither your politics nor the politics of those with you, and I have no wish to argue with you anymore. You are no longer my kind of person." Or perhaps not, perhaps she was done with Benjamin. There were so many others, young men and women, queuing up to sit at her feet—and if none had his gifts, which once chimed so sympathetically with her own, well—she shrugged and hauled herself to her feet. And now the letters were getting in her way, his and everyone else's, so many of them, in boxes stacked around her desk—she knocked one over and the contents were strewn across the floor. Wasn't she hemmed in by so much past?

The irresistible pull of the couch in the late afternoon. She'd abandon the struggle for now—to write, to keep her eyes open. Another half-hour and Ruth would bring the tea things, and find her stretched out under her plaid rug, asleep.

I'm thinking now about spaces. Ideal spaces, to live in, to live a perfect life in, to be calm and good in. I'm thinking of a place without particular entrances or exits, in which spaces take the place of rooms, spaces that emerge out of and into other spaces, that are shaped rather than angled, curved rather than cornered, some inside and some out; in which windows and doors are set wherever there's a notable view, of gardens tended or city streets, or the light is especially advantageous. These spaces have no particular functions, and a person might lie down to sleep on one of several daybeds, sit down to eat or work at any of the many tables. A stove in the centre of one of these spaces would supply heat and cooking facilities, and a bathroom, placed at one or other end of the sequence, would take a more pronounced curve so as to be made private. Gentle, organic, continuous forms, snaking across landscapes, would make for a world without beginnings or endings, starts or stops, or wieldings of power and possession—on and on and on.

PART TWO

THE WAY WE LOVED

MEMORY, OR DREAM?

I'm sitting with my brother Hugo in the back of a car parked in a layby. In the dying light he is no more than a dim, perhaps sleeping shadow beside me for I'm absorbed by the scene outside. My mother and father—and a policeman in an unfamiliar flat hat. My father says something to the policeman, who shrugs in a desultory way and glances towards the road as if he's expecting something. My mother stands apart, on the side of the lay-by away from the road, at the edge of a rocky ravine. We're in the mountains and Simon, my younger brother, is lost. My mother holds a pair of binoculars to her eyes and is scanning the mountainside. I can't see her face but I know from the tense way she holds her shoulders that she's desperately worried.

A black car turns into the layby and stops abruptly. The back door swings open. Hands are reaching for a child who is half clambering, half lifted over knees. I wait for the child to declare itself, but my father shows no such caution. He is bounding towards the car, reaching out to receive the child—and blocks my view. My mother has lowered the binoculars and watches the drama of Simon's return with a curious detachment. Hugo, beside me, begins to whimper, a sound that plucks at my nerves like a lost thought.

A memory? Or a dream—recurring so often at one time that it has taken its place alongside all the other stories that explain us.

I save what I've written and shuffle stiffly over to the window. The puffy white sky reflects the blanket of snow that drapes the square, softening and blurring the shapes of things—trees, cars, railings. It's been snowing all day, the heaviest snowfall since the winter of my birth, when—as my mother told it—it was difficult to keep a baby warm in the draughty rooms of our house in Hampstead, with gas fires that barely took the chill off.

In the childhood of my memory snow came every winter. Waking to the blanched light and muffled sounds that told of a snowfall over night, I would run to the window and marvel at the transformed world outside, eager for the pleasures to come, the dry smell of it and the smooth perfection that awaited spoiling with the first imprint of my booted feet.

A snowstorm: I sat in the back of the car beside Hugo, and the snow whirled furiously all around us. I was excited until something changed, I felt a tension in my parents, and then the spinning flakes ceased to be a thrill, and my excitement slipped into fear.

My mother, the driver in the family, was hunched over the wheel, peering through the windscreen in an attempt to see out. Beside her, my father studied a map, a rustling sheet on his lap, but then threw up his hands in frustration and muttered: "Next to useless." And started telling my mother what to do as the car began to slide and slip.

"I can't …" she said.

"Can't what?" Hugo struggled to get out of his harness. "Can't what?"

"Quiet," snapped my father.

But I knew what, because the car came to a shuddering stop as it banged against another. The first suggestion that my parents weren't omnipotent, that things could go wrong in ways that were beyond their control.

Then I'm sitting in front of my father on a sledge, and his arms are round me. As we toboggan ever faster down the steep gradient of our street I feel an intense, ecstatic joy.

A young woman visited us, Victor and me. She brought a baby with her, a little boy, still at the breast. How he sucked! Great gulping sounds, and then he'd break off, distracted, only to return after a moment with renewed vigour. His mother followed his cues, offering her breast when he wanted to suck, withdrawing when he'd had enough. He owned those breasts, hitting them and biting them, and grabbing at them; he did as he wanted with them. I too had fed at my mother's breast but something had compromised our intimacy.

In photographs she holds me away from her body, at a distance and a little stiffly, as if offering me to the camera. Or I sit upright on her lap and she regards me with an expression that's quizzical, unillusioned. Contrast this with how her arms envelop my brother Hugo, and how she meets his gaze, in a reverie of love. There's nothing I want more than to be held in those arms, to meet that gaze; I gasp at the intensity of my desire. Perhaps in me she saw her own reflection, and didn't like the sight. Or is this to see it with the bias of a later resentment? I was a prickly baby, so it was said. I would scream if an unknown face peered down at me in my cot. My mother's expression may be wary, knowing that the smallest wrong move would likely set me off.

Tragedy had attended my mother's birth to a mother who survived for only ten days. No one spoke of her—my grandfather was said to be inconsolable—but certain facts her daughters knew: she was born in Dublin and named Peggy, she hoped to be a pianist, but died aged 26, leaving the baby Beatrice (my mother) and her sister Vera, who was then eighteen months old. They knew, too, what she looked like from a photograph that hung in their bedroom: a haze of dark hair, a smile that held something back, but a face too young to be marked by life, without presentiment.

Vera claimed to remember her.

"The sea's lapping at my feet and her skirt's blowing everywhere and I get caught in it and she bends down and disentangles me."

"Don't tell it so quickly": Beatrice.

"Her face is upside down. She picks me up."

"And then?"

"I can't remember."

"I think it was Jess."

"It wasn't."

"You can't really remember. Who you think was her was Jess and I remember her too."

Cousin Jess came from Ireland for Peggy's second confinement and stayed on after her death to care for the two little girls—until sacked, five years later, by their new stepmother. Jess claimed to be packing for a holiday at home in Dublin, but the tears in her eyes belied her story, and Vera, always the sharp one, began to suspect. When the cab came, Beatrice, highly strung and sensing disaster, threw herself down on the hall floor and, screaming all the while, banged her head again and again on the door mat. Thus she missed the actual leave-taking that was no such thing. Jess, herself distraught (sobbing, according to Vera, who apparently remembered), left without saying goodbye.

"I'll never forget it." Vera warmed to her story. "Jess stumbled down the steps and dashed into the car. I ran after her, tried to get in too—"

"You didn't. You've never told me that before. I bet you're making it up."

"I thought about it. But then I realised it wouldn't be fair to leave you behind."

"I'd have had Daddy."

"Daddy would have been devastated."

"At your going away with Jess? No he wouldn't. He'd have laughed at your audacity and fetched you home."

And then the aftermath, as I picture it: their stepmother (they learnt to call her Ma, to us grand-children she was Nana), shaken perhaps by the storm of emotion she had unleashed, and not impervious, unusually sat with them at tea. Vera, pale, silent, unbending, declined a conciliatory offer of an extra slice of cake—but Beatrice, always willing to give a person the benefit of the doubt, and cleansed by her fit of hysterics, not to say greedy for cake, held out her plate gratefully, and ignored Vera's sharp kick on her ankle.

"She was always conscientious," my mother would say of our Nana. "She made sure we went to the dentist, that sort of thing, but she was a jealous woman and should never have been a second wife." "A stepmother has to love her stepchildren as her own." Nana didn't, she loved only Marion—if "love" was the word for the suffocating possessiveness that prevented her from seeing any wrong in her own daughter, made her deaf and blind to the love claims of her step-daughters. "Spoilt," my mother said of her half-sister Marion, "but in a way she was as starved of decent mother's-love as we were."

A photograph may show how it was between the sisters— Vera and Beatrice, and their half-sister Marion. They sit on a bench. Marion, on the right, is playing to the camera, laughing, squirming, full-face, while Beatrice (my mother), in the middle, leans slightly towards her older sister Vera, on the left, and away from Marion. The two older girls bend their heads to the side self-deprecatingly, and though they smile they do so in a way that holds something back, as if they've learnt to be wary of the world. Clothes also connect the older two: identical coats tied rather shapelessly at the waist, thick stockings, and laced-up walking shoes. Marion looks smartly dressed by comparison—her socks are taut, not wrinkled as the stockings of the other two are, the coat is tightly belted round the slim waist, a striped skirt visible below. Her blond hair is swept back from her face, helped by the wind. It's not a pretty face but it's lively, while the faces of the older girls are decent but dour. These two are unmistakably sisters: the same round faces, the same shadow of sadness. Marion doesn't look sad, she looks as if everything has always gone her way.

I'm seeing the photograph through the prism of my mother's grievance. But if Marion seems to be calling for attention, who does she want it from? Perhaps it hasn't dawned on her yet that the other two have punished her with exclusion, that she'll never broach the defences they've erected against her. No wonder that as soon as she can she will flee to America, bride of a US airman.

My mother's face crumpled, the fat tears began to flow. That was before the accident and may have had something to do with how my father slammed the front door on our departing backs. I didn't see the cyclist emerge from a side road, but I saw my mother's doleful expression suddenly animated by alarm as she stamped on the brake. We lurched forwards, heard the thump—and my brothers, in the back, began to wail.

She got out and keeping the open car door between her and the cyclist peered down at him on the ground. "Oh, have you hurt your poor leg?" The softly voiced enquiry seemed inappropriately restrained. Something more urgent would have suited the situation better. I worried too that the prostrated cyclist might object that it was my mother who had hurt his leg. But the policeman didn't think so. He was on her side, told her to go home and make herself a cup of tea.

And then it was the next day and we were convalescing in the garden when Nana suddenly appeared round the side of the house, an unexpected visitor. She came to comfort my mother who got up hesitantly, as if she was taken aback by Nana's arrival. She walked across the garden, and in her oddly bowed head I recognised the signs that she was crying. Nana took her by the arm and led her gently into the house. My mother wept perhaps for the love that, unfettered by history and flaws in character, might have burgeoned between them.

My mother remembered how as a child she would knock on Nana's door and if she was in the mood Nana might tell her things, but only if Marion was out of the way. Favourites may insist on their privileges but they aren't always kind to those who favour them—Vera to Beatrice no less than Marion to her mother. Beatrice learnt to keep quiet about these times with Nana. Vera, who directed her daughterly feelings only to their father, saw them as a betrayal. She called them crumbs of comfort. But Beatrice wouldn't give them up.

In my mother's opinion I had the best of Nana. She called me her pin-up girl. Sometimes I try to conjure her—a commanding presence, a deep voice and hoot of laughter, and the smell of her rose-scented powder. We would sit, one on either side of the fire in the parlour off the hall in her house, Nana in her wing-backed chair, me on the couch opposite, sipping our evening drinks (mine ginger ale, hers whisky) and talking—but then she fades like a ghost in a thick grey miasma.

One time, Nana had been quiet, somehow dejected or distracted. She'd remarked several times on the oppressive greyness of those February days which seemed to last forever. "The worst month," she said. "How I hate February."

"Sometimes it's like spring."

"A false spring. Don't let it fool you."

I didn't know this tone of hers—bitter, scornful of herself, as if she'd been taken in by false springs and the cost was great.

"Not that I blame the weather."

I waited, not liking to ask what or who she blamed, or for what, watching as she stared into the fire until, as if to herself, she said: "There's no denying the date"—and explained how she had lost her fiancé in the first war, in the cruel false spring of 1917.

Friends had counselled her against marriage to my grand-father. But what they saw as an impediment—his evident grief for the mother of his little girls—she saw as their common ground. And there weren't many suitors. How could there be?—after the slaughter of young men in that war.

My mother told me that when my grandfather came to inspect me shortly after my birth, he took out his pocket watch, opened up the back, where he kept a photograph of his first wife Peggy. He held it against my face, hoping to see her like-ness in me, his (and her) first granddaughter. He did this in the presence of Nana, whose face could never match up with mine (even if it was possible to see Peggy's angular beauty in a baby's podgy creases), thus underlining her second-bestness. Neither he, it seems, nor my mother in the telling, gave any thought to Nana. Nor did anyone think of me, implicated within days of my birth in the family drama. Did I sense my grandfather's disappointed grimace as he snapped shut the back of the pocket watch?—which was registered, my mother said, both the grimace and the snap, by Nana with an uncon-trolled jerk of her head.

Such stories formed my imaginative landscape; my own experiences paled before my mother's. But I loved her recita-tions, the intimacy of her confidences, when our feelings for each other felt strong and true.

We were travelling on a train once, sitting side by side in a compartment that was empty except for a man in the far cor-ner seat with a file of papers. Every so often he would look up and stare at my mother as she spoke, compulsively, of her childhood, unaware of everything in the present, even me her daughter who sat beside her as her sounding board. I was often on the verge of tears—would feel them welling up, and put on my dark glasses to hide my emotion from our fellow traveller.

I remember very little of my mother's outpourings, though I suspect that much of what I know of her first years I learnt then: Nana's severity, particularly to Vera, so special to their

88

father; Nana's favouring Marion; the silence that reigned on the subject of Vera and Beatrice's true mother Peggy; my grandfather's unassuaged grief, his infidelities, and Nana's unhappinesses, her crush on the family doctor—my mother said what she had to relate with a monotonous, hypnotic insistence, as if she was expelling demons, but knew not that she did so.

As I got older my mother would find fault with me, objecting to my demeanour, to what she saw as my supercilious attitude. Sometimes she announced to my brothers that I was to be sent to Coventry, for a crime that wasn't always made clear. Later still, she would push me forward to take her place as my father's companion at events she didn't want to attend. She said it was my duty to support him—as if she, his wife, had no such obligation. There was an office party, and visits to the theatre. I also remember being alone with him in a restaurant, I've forgotten why. A band was playing and he persuaded me to dance. I felt embarrassed by the way people smiled at us, at the touching sight of a middle-aged man dancing a waltz with his young daughter—also by the thought that some must surely have thought it odd, as I did, and would have looked at us askance.

He took me once to the village where his grandmother had lived, and where he'd been happy as a boy, happier than in his own home, where a younger brother had died in childhood (their mother's favourite, so my father believed). I remember a broad, sloping green and picturesque cottages round it. And a picnic by a stream. A perfect June day and a shady meadow and cows across the water munching the long grass. My father put a bottle of beer in the stream, balancing it between two stones, to keep it cool.

We sat by the stream and ate our picnic and talked of this and that, so easily in those days. And when we'd eaten he said, "Let's have a snooze," and he lay down on the grass. "Rest your head here," he said, in an uprush of feeling I think, nothing more, and so as not to break the spell I rested my head where he asked, on his belly, and we lay there looking up at the leaves fluttering and rustling as if whispering to one another. I felt awkward, wanting to get up but not wanting to offend him, and all the time he lay quietly content, his head on his crossed arms—until the sound of glass against stone allowed me to jump up and save his beer.

My mother greeted us resentfully when we got back, said she felt like the *au pair*, left behind to keep an eye on the other children.

One day, I sat beside him in the car—wearing my best dress—and my mother stood at the open window on my side and, shouting across me at my father, told him she was going to divorce him. I felt implicated, if only by dint of being in the car with him and going somewhere in a red dress, in which he'd told me I looked pretty, rather than on the pavement with my mother who was going nowhere, and had given up on best dresses and compliments from my father. I think it was then that I decided to hide my love for him. It seemed the only way out, to stop my mother's jealousy, to heal their rift, but instead it brought complaints from my father, who called me cold and sulky.

Lying on my bed, scrunched up tight in a ball, I hugged myself for comfort. I cried for hours. My mother came at last, as I hoped she would, and then my father, but though they were clearly shaken, they never broke our silence.

"Clown," I whispered to myself, "you clown." And then: "Poor clown, poor clown, poor, poor clown."

My brother Hugo held nothing against our parents: they had their frailties but he understood how they came by them, they did the best they could, and ours had been a happy childhood. "There were many happinesses," he said, "many kindnesses"— and he began to list the picnics and birthday parties, the

Christmas stockings and seaside holidays. "But that isn't what you mean," he said, catching a sceptical look on my face.

Did he remember, I asked him, that time we were all in the car? Unusually, our father was at the wheel, my mother next to him, and the three children behind. Our parents were arguing, about the route perhaps, or my father's erratic driving, which my mother, always very nervous and managing in the passenger's seat, never hesitated to criticise. At a certain point my father, exasperated and angry, lashed out at her, hitting her above the eye with his fist. After a moment's shocked silence, she started to cry.

Yes, Hugo said, he did remember; also how later she supplied us with an explanation for her black eye: "I walked into a door": said firmly, as if she could wipe out memory by a tone of voice.

My father's attacks of rage were startling in a man of such loving kindness. Perhaps his anger had something to do with the war, that as a pilot he had dropped bombs on the Japanese occupiers of Burmese villages and presumably on the people who lived in them too. And though he found a way to do it, sooner or later he'd have had to think about it. Perhaps he didn't share my mother's view, that they'd been blessed by a special grace. He'd survived the war and she hadn't expected him to, the odds were against it, a pilot's survival. Perhaps he began to question the justice of it. And just as my mother ceased to recognise the young man she had marked out on a troopship—straining to read Herodotus under a poor light amidst a mob of soldiers—so too did my father lose sight of the self he believed to be true, burdened as he was by memories and the need to earn a living for his family.

There came a time when, if they spoke at all, my parents were bound to quarrel. Mostly they played out their enmity at the ritual of Sunday lunch. A joint of meat was always on the menu, and pudding, which my mother spent the morning preparing. Only my father and Hugo were interested in the food. Simon was a vegetarian, and I was too nervous to notice what I was swallowing, while my mother, having prepared the meal, was probably tempted to take a sandwich up to her room. But, as it was, she sat down, and my father carved. He found fault with her cooking—she tended to overcook, and burnt things. Then there was the absence more often than not of what my father regarded as essential condiments. Lamb was inedible without redcurrant jelly and mint sauce; pork must have apple sauce; beef, horseradish. And rice pudding needed raspberry jam. My mother couldn't see the point, unless she was simply registering rebellion against my father's absurdly exacting requirements. In any case these banalities triggered other clashes. Her superior class and wealth often came up between them, but the fact was they had come to disappoint one another and themselves.

My task as I saw it was to deflect them with conversation, being careful not to make cultural or intellectual references that would bore my mother, which meant thwarting my father's tendency to address all his remarks to me. The vigilance required to distract them was a matter of juggling, keeping the balls in play with each so they couldn't sabotage one another's conversation. But if people are intent on fighting, they can't be stopped, and sooner or later, defeated, I would drop my mask and retreat into silence as my mother fled the room in tears. My father, head down, would grimly finish his meal before also retreating to his room. Hugo and Simon sloped off somewhere. We were all too ashamed to look one another in the eye.

Then I'm eighteen, and in Nana's room the bed was stripped and the windows were wide open as if she had flown away. A baby cried. I looked out and saw in the garden next door a woman on a swing trying to pacify a child in arms. I watched them, aware that I too ought to weep, for Nana, who lay dying in the hospital, and wondered that I didn't, that however sad I didn't just burst into tears as the baby did.

I lay down on the bare mattress to await aunt Marion—I'd been assigned to greet her on her arrival from America. As I dozed, voices came to me, the sounds of children at play, as had happened to me before in that house, Nana's, and my mother's home as a child:

- *I'm Beatrice Todd. Tell me I'm going to be a pianist like my mother.*
- *That won't work. You're doing it wrong. You mustn't want anything. You've got to be neutral.*
- *Please tell me I'm going to be a pianist.*
- *No. Tell me what I'm going to be.*
- *Nothing's happening.*
- *It's your fault. You did it wrong.*
- *I don't believe in it anyway. I don't need anyone to tell me I'm going to be a pianist. I am one.*
- *You'll never be allowed. Oh look who's here. What do you want, Marion?*
- *I don't have to want anything. I live here. What are you doing?*
- *Clearing up the cards:* Beatrice.
- *You've been talking to the spirits. Does Ma know?*
- *Tell-tale tit:* Vera.

Soon I got up and wandered downstairs. In the drawing room I approached the piano my mother had once played. The mechanism for altering the height of the stool had broken many years before, and because her father and Nana had felt that to mend the stool would be to overvalue her playing, she had always sat on a pile of music. I turned the pages of a Bach fugue propped on the music stand and thought of my mother's dashed dreams.

I switched on the television and watched a news report from Paris. Students had constructed sixty barricades around the rue Gay-Lussac, holding the Latin Quarter for several hours against the police with their clubs and tear gas. May 1968. A student leader explained that their revolution invited everyone to stop being onlookers and to release their own creativity. "Who wants to do boring work just to earn a rotten living?" "Down with work!" he cried, suddenly raising his voice. "Free the passions!" "Live without wasted time!"

I would have done well to pay attention, but at that time my heart and mind were engaged elsewhere, for it was then that I held an almost nightly vigil outside a house in Cambridge Gardens, a street, with its peeling stucco and reek of cats, that I would forever after associate with a state of despair pierced by moments of ecstasy, that particular mood of spring and youth, febrile yet torpid, and directionless. That was a time, apparently, when I had nothing better to do with the hours of twilight than stand and wait under a tree, watching the house, and hearing the rumble of tube trains, above ground at that point, as they left or entered Ladbroke Grove station.

Gough, my college tutor, lived in the house. I'd seen him once, when he appeared at the bay window with a book in his hands and peered out as if he was expecting someone. When he glanced in my direction I jumped like a hare—but he didn't see me in the shadow of the tree, and turned back into the room and was lost to view.

I suppose I thought I hoped to see him again, even to speak to him, but every time it was a relief that I didn't, as if I knew that no dream of perfect love could possibly come true from such a shaming encounter.

I began to sing. On the landing above the hall, for no particular reason, because it wasn't my birthday, I sang "Happy Birthday" to myself. When I reached the final "dear Lin" I launched my voice into a descant to execute many exaggerated trills. And when I'd finished I bowed deeply as if to an audience that

94

had assembled below at the first sound of my voice and as I finished broke spontaneously into applause.

The sound of a scuffle on the front steps alerted me to the arrival of Marion. She immediately seemed to fill the house with her brittle, restless presence, whipping up its gentle currents so that I too felt jangled and displaced.

"Where is everyone?"

"They're at the hospital."

"And left you on your own?" Marion embraced me and murmured, "Oh poor dear Lin—and poor Ma." She wept lightly for a moment, her head on my shoulder. Then she seemed to give herself a shake. "No good blubbering," and blew her nose. She made a pirouette round the hall and into the parlour, where she switched on the light and, standing at the door, said: "Whatever happened to my Dresden lady?"

The Dresden lady: a porcelain shepherdess that always stood on Nana's mantelpiece. I remembered a recent conversation between my mother and her sister Vera—

"She wants it," Vera reported.

"Well, can't she have it?"

"Of course she can't," Vera said. "It's mine."

I didn't know what reply to give to Marion's question and fortunately she answered it herself: "Vera has taken it. She's always had her eye on it, but only because I loved it, and it was my mother's and was always going to be mine." Marion's voice rose high and screechy; I heard the emphasis in "*my* mother", the possession her sisters couldn't forgive her for.

In a touching photograph of my mother as a child she crouches beside her dog, her hands cupping his face, and looks deeply and adoringly into his eyes. After her children left home she transferred her affections back to her dogs—her first love, and her last.

My father bought Algie after the family dog died, to soften the blow for my mother. But Algie attached himself to my father, and it wasn't long before my mother went to the dogs' home and came back with Freddie. The adoption, as my mother called it, of a mongrel looked like a reproach to my father—for buying a dog, and for buying one that liked him more than her. She wouldn't dream, she said, of buying a pedigree dog when the world was full of abandoned, unloved dogs like Freddie—who could only be seen as a judgement on my father and the perfectly bred Algie.

Next, my mother acquired Zanzibar, and my father retreated in defeat to his room, abandoning Algie in the process. It was as if by bringing a third dog into the house my mother upset their uneasy balance. Algie, Freddie, Zanzie became, all three, my mother's dogs, though Algie's position was always vulnerable and insufficiently protected. Poor Algie would sometimes be found at my father's closed door, sitting like a sentinel, as if guarding him against the others' predations, or perhaps pathetically hoping to be let into safety by his erstwhile master. I too sometimes felt I'd been delivered by my father into my mother's erratic possession.

But I felt her poignancy too. I remember a remark she once made about playing the piano: "I don't know what I do it for"—and I felt the anguish that would have given rise to her self-questioning. As if activities had to have a point, a usefulness, and what was the good in playing the piano if one didn't give other people pleasure or instruction? That one might do something just because one enjoyed it was a difficult idea for my mother to accept. Perhaps she kept dogs because they had to be cared for and sustained; they gave her something useful to do as playing the piano or even practising the piano did not.

ADRIAN

"I hate him, I hate him, I hate him." I swigged back the final dregs of wine in my glass and contemplated the coils of slimy spaghetti congealed on my plate with blobs of winter nitrate lettuce, my nightly fare, picked up at the shop round the corner from the house I lodged in, in Bayswater. Sometimes it seemed like love. I tried it out: "I love him"— and would have liked to turn the table over, cast the disgusting remains of my meal across the room. Instead I sat down at my desk and reached for pen and paper. *Dear Adrian*—I wrote— *From the day we first met I felt an unusual*—I paused—*regard*—I struck out *regard*, tried *affection*, struck that out and tried *regard* again—*regard for you. That's why it's particularly painful to have to explain*—I struck out *explain*—wrote *announce*—and paused. "Announce what?" I said out loud. *My despair, disregard, engagement, love*, no, not *love, my vulnerability, I have to announce*, no, *warn*—or *inform*—*I have to inform you that I find your behaviour objectionable and attach no importance whatsoever to your little acts of flirtatiousness.*

Oh, but I did. I loved him. But I also hated him—and wanted to kneel astride him and fuck him hard.

I worked for Adrian at a publisher's office in Harrow. From the beginning, even at my interview, his manner implied a flattering but dangerous collusion which made me hesitate to take the job. Was it the familiarity of his teasing tone (so like my father's)? Or perhaps the presence of a pale, unsmiling woman with carroty hair, called Susan, who sat at a desk next to his, like a gatekeeper, watching us sardonically and smoking.

I was told that Adrian had taken up with Susan after his marriage failed. Someone in the office knew his wife. "She had intellectual interests but left him." That's how this person put it—he liked her seriousness but then she did this stupid thing of leaving Adrian. I too thought it was a stupid thing to do, though I would come to understand it only too well—how he got under one's skin and manipulated one's feelings, seemed to promise everything and never followed through.

I've questioned myself closely about my own behaviour. Did I respond to his suggestiveness? Did I even provoke him?—*was I culpable?* Or did he flirt with every woman he encountered, which Susan's air of indulgent martyrdom suggested? Was I special, in other words, as I came to believe, or just another object in the service of his vanity?

And what was I to make of his insinuations? Did he think I didn't notice how he caused me to brush his hand when he passed me something? In my nervousness, my hand shook and when it touched his he snatched it away as if I was about to jump on him. And when he came over to my desk to say something he stood too close, intruding into my space, so that I was forced to push back my chair out of the way. He liked too to fix his gaze on my breast or knee just long enough for me to register it. And he did these things only in the office, where the presence of others forestalled any possibility of a declaration. In more appropriate settings he ignored me. At an office party, for instance, when we might have talked, he didn't even catch my eye. It was as if he denied the conclusion everything in his behaviour at the office was bound to suggest. His seduction seemed to have no other aim but to enslave me.

I crumpled up my letter to Adrian and threw it across the room in the direction of the waste-paper basket. I took another piece and wrote to my brother. *Dear Simon, it's late after a hard day and I won't say much, just that I'm sorry not to have come to see you off to Australia but it's impossible to take leave from work just now, or even if it isn't, I seem unable to drag myself away. I hope you had a safe journey. Love from Lin.* I read it through and changed *safe journey* to *propitious arrival*. Even I, with thought for little else besides my own petty concerns, would probably have noticed the headlines reporting a plane crash. Or my mother would have phoned me at work—I imagined her hysterical tears and then my father's voice as he took the phone and said calmly, wearily that Simon's plane had gone down. I felt tears in my eyes, but quickly shook my head—no nonsense—and addressed an envelope.

Working lovingly, slavishly for Adrian, I lived for moments when, as we pored over a text, I believed that he loved me as I loved him and was for some reason biding his time before declaring himself. I didn't consider his apparent commitment to Susan; she was not, to my deluded eye, a serious rival.

Then, one Saturday morning, on the way to work, I encountered a young girl weeping in a doorway in Praed Street. I took her to a café; she ate a huge breakfast and told me her story. She was 16, from Bournemouth, and running away from a boyfriend who abused her (she showed me burn marks on her arms). She had a baby, looked after by her mother, who had herself been a single parent. Natalie—that was her name— had a girlfriend in London who had offered to put her up. At the prospect of a new adventure she forgot her sadness and brightened up, eager to find her friend. After she'd gone I resumed my journey to work but suddenly it seemed absurd to go to the office on a Saturday, when I didn't have to, and I turned back. It was as if Natalie had enabled me to breech my own subjection—to the extent that a few days later I gave in my notice to Adrian.

He took me out to dinner to talk me out of it—without much difficulty. We went to a restaurant owned by some friends of his, and I had the feeling he was using me to make a point—here he was, still capable of attracting a younger woman. He said nothing personal to me, about his circumstances, about his wife or Susan. It was a very ambiguous occasion, and I didn't know where I stood. He was worried about finishing the project and asked me to stay six months longer. It seemed mean and unsatisfactory not to agree, and intolerably sad. He drove me home afterwards and when he got out of the car to say goodbye he put out an arm to me and I dodged it. He was untouchable, it seemed, except in my imaginings of our passion, no longer fantasies of angry, aggressive sex but of gentle nibbling little kisses and deep, tender embraces, our hearts full of love.

It was around that time that Victor, a childhood friend of my brother Hugo, sent me one of his occasional cards. *Dear Lin*, he wrote. *Please forgive my silence. Perhaps I should have written to explain. I felt, like Parsifal, I'd failed to ask the Questions—and somehow felt acutely uncomfortable and shifty in your presence even while liking you and respecting you very much. And then everything became so terribly hurried and demanding, so that only the firmest, oldest, most urgent friendships got cultivated. Now things are quieter again. Perhaps we'd better meet initially not tête-à-tête. Victor.*

He was referring to the most recent of our persistent but inconclusive attempts to see through our long-term interest in one another. I can't remember how I responded but I must have suggested a meeting, though my heart wasn't in it, since this was his reply: *Dear Lin, just in case I fail to reach you by phone I'm afraid Saturday is impossible. Often it's a difficult day for me since it can be complicated by getting down here on a Sunday, and Monday is my main lecturing day. I leave for Africa early next month.*

Looking forward to seeing you when I return. Victor—followed a few months later by: *Dear Lin, I'm now in the second month of this adventure. Let's hope to meet next year. Victor.*

For a time my hopes that Adrian reciprocated my love were rekindled, and I was able to bury my insight that what I thought I wanted could and would never happen. But the sense of hopelessness returned, and with it the desolation that followed from what felt like a rejection of my finest feelings. Eventually, buried in some deep internal place, I found the spirit to save myself, and left Adrian. This time he didn't try to dissuade me but took me out for a farewell lunch.

I couldn't eat anything. When I tried to swallow a morsel of food it stuck in my gullet. It seemed important to tell him at last that I loved him. Somehow I had to speak the words, and I managed it, I got them out. He said he had wondered, and that he "admired" me, but he was seeing someone else as well as Susan, and any other attachment was out of the question. He was sad and regretful but also, in his own eyes, blameless: he reminded me of the time we'd had dinner together, how he had reached out to me and I had flinched. As if my coldness then had sealed my fate.

Afterwards I walked to the station and was assailed by the finality of what I'd done. It was like a death. As if he had died. I couldn't bring myself to get on a train that would take me away from him, finally, forever. I walked back in the direction of the office, but didn't go in. I walked in the streets, I don't know for how long, but at last I left. Already I was composing the letter I would write in hope of changing his mind, so that he would come to acknowledge his love for me and there'd be an end to my unbearable feelings of loss.

A couple of years later I saw him in the street. He was hurrying, as if he was late for an appointment, and as he walked he ran a comb through his hair in a familiar gesture. I didn't hail him because I didn't feel able just then to give a good account of myself. I never saw him again, but someone I knew in those days wrote in a Christmas card that he'd met Adrian somewhere and he'd asked for news of me. I hadn't heard from this former colleague for many years, and I didn't hear again, and I wondered why he had bothered to relay what was no more than a passing enquiry.

Whenever I visited my parents in those years, the Adrian years, I felt like a criminal compelled to return to the scene of her crime. I couldn't keep away from a situation that had formed, and distorted, me. My father seemed remote, and if I joined them for supper he would swallow down his food and as soon as he'd finished go to his room. My mother and I, drinking too much wine, sat on. I spoke little, torn between feelings of guilt, believing I must make amends to her, and anger because I'd suffered at her hands. Perhaps the habit of silence, which was ingrained in me, had even become a revenge—for she longed to be the recipient of my secrets.

Instead we spoke of Simon. She worried about his welfare, imagining what could go wrong in Australia—all the more since he rarely replied to our letters, which we posted rather as one might cast a message in a bottle into the sea, to whomever it may concern.

My mother was also troubled by a bad internal pain. She found it difficult to get comfortable—even reading was painful, and the worst thing of all was walking her three dogs, though it was as if they knew she was hurt, she said, and tried not to pull on their leads.

At the start of her illness my father walked the dogs, but as the weeks passed he would just open the back door to let them roam in the garden. So Hugo and I took it in turns to walk them. On my first outing, their leads became entangled in one another and in my hands and round my legs, and it took twenty minutes when it should have taken five to get along the street and across the main road into the park. As we crossed the road, one of the dogs, poor old Algie, stopped to sniff a clump in the zebra crossing and an approaching motorist had to slam on his breaks to avoid running us all down. Then it was the usual nightmare of getting the dogs to follow me once they'd been let off their leads, and attaching them again when it was time to go home. After that I walked the dogs up and down the street rather than in the park and, as if to punish me, they peed and shat on the pavement or against people's cars instead of neatly in the gutter.

SEA AIR

I switched off the engine and my father clambered out, gingerly straightening his back, which always troubled him on a long car journey. He walked round to my mother's door to give her a hand. Neither of them drove anymore, my father having acknowledged at last that he was dangerous behind a wheel, and my mother because she was poorly. The treatment had made an old woman of her, not in the face but in her tottering, shuffling body, in her querulous voice and tearfulness. Sitting beside me on the journey to Frinton, from time to time she wept. And when my father reached forward from the back and clasped her shoulder she shrugged him off, as if he was the last person with the right to console her. I sensed his shrinking into the corner of his seat and in the mirror saw him purse his lips to suppress a hurt or an irritable retort. But perhaps it wasn't my father she shrugged off but the tears, which came for no particular reason and of their own accord, a side-effect of illness. I prayed she would take his proffered arm, and not brush him off again. And she did, grasping it with both hands.

She stood for a moment, looking at the house, lent by a friend, as if it might offer salvation. Our eyes, my father's and mine, followed her gaze expectantly.

"All I need," she said, "is a lungful of sea air."

I placed a deckchair beneath an apple tree where she might rest, lulled by the greenish light and the distant sounds of the beach—children calling and the rhythmic clatter of pebbles dragged by the sea. "Didn't I say?" she asked as my father draped a shawl over her knees. "The sea will do the trick." There was nothing else she wanted but to lie under a tree, with the prospect of a gentle stroll to the beach.

It couldn't be said that we strolled down to the front next morning because my mother was frail and clung to me. I felt awkward, so long was it since I'd held her, or she had held me. But when we reached a bench overlooking the sea and I let go of her, I felt the loss. She sat on the cushion I'd carried for her and in spite of the sun drew her linen coat close. She was more than usually tired from the journey and a night in a strange bed.

She closed her eyes and lifted her face to the sun. I thought how like a child she looked. But then she seemed to age, as if her whole life, decade by decade, was playing itself out across her features, which blurred and drooped and spread as the years rolled by.

We ate lunch in the garden, at a table on the patio. My mother still loved her food. She told the old story of how her nanny had said she was so greedy she'd be eating a banquet on her death bed. It seemed to be so.

I found being with them both the usual strain. My father told us about the book he was reading and I listened and then questioned him. My mother, bored, started asking me questions about my life. He talked on regardless, asking me whether I knew the work of the poet who was the subject of the book. I said I didn't, smiling at my mother and then at my father, saying something to one and then to the other, and in the end my father got up and left the table.

My mother rested in the garden after lunch. My father and I read in our rooms. At teatime, I wandered through the darkened house, curtained against the heat of the sun. I stepped out through the French windows and on to the patio and blinked in the sudden glare of white light. My mother called to me. "I'd forgotten you were here, then I heard your step. What a joy!" Her voice trembled on the verge of tears and my eyes flooded, but then she stiffened, remembering that she had to be brave, we all had to be brave and pretend, each for the sake of the others.

"I've got a plan," she confided, her face round and smooth, her blue eyes bright. She had always loved a project, and would throw herself into it regardless of anyone who stood in her way. "Don't tell your father," she whispered, "I haven't mentioned it to him yet."

She had decided to move house. "Not now. When I'm better. Next spring I should think." She wanted a view of the river. Chiswick perhaps or Hammersmith, not Barnes, she'd never liked south of the Thames, which reminded her of a childhood agony, returning from a weekend in the country with her father and sister, the endless drive through the suburbs, feelings of dread growing all the time until they crossed Chelsea Bridge, when a sense of resignation set in. To what? To their stepmother's chilly domain.

"Something easy to run." Housework was a thing of the past. "When I think of all the yellow dusters I've washed and hung out on the line. Do you know, in the hospital the cleaners used disposable wipes. Just threw them away. Yes, a small modern flat. With a view of the river."

Later, I watched from the living-room window as she set out with my father on a little stroll. He had an arm round her, and her coat was ruffled where he clasped her hip. They walked very slowly, heads together. My father raised an arm to gesture at something and they stopped. My mother laughed. She took his arm, and they walked on, companionable and resolute. I felt a moment's anguish at my exclusion and almost called after them to take me too. But then an image came to me of wide vistas opening up before me, a vision of distant horizons and boundless skies. It seemed to me then that I would never understand all the peculiar ambivalences, the hatred and love, the pain and grief that lay between them. It was their story, not mine—and there was some relief in that conclusion; I felt returned to myself, a free agent. But I also felt bereft, as if the veil protecting me from a full view of our reality had been cruelly snatched away.

My father and I planned her funeral. Sitting side by side at the dining-room table, we arranged the details of her cremation. It was as if I had triumphed. And in the evening after the funeral, which was like a party, I might have been celebrating my triumph. But I felt neither triumphant nor celebratory.

Hugo and a cousin were talking as I cut up the pizza. My father, who had broken down at the ceremony, was calm now, half listening to them as he poured some wine, good wine, to add to the party feeling. They were talking about the Falklands. I felt uneasy because I knew it would remind my father, that talk, as it reminded me, how much the war upset her. In fact, in my view, it killed her. Among other things, I dare say, and everyone's got their opinion—too much wine, not enough carrots—but I think, more than anything it was the Falklands war, and whatever it was that the war meant to her, the absence that was almost a loss of a son perhaps. Of Simon. Was it that?

She talked of little else at the time, not only at home so my father became irritated, but in the street to strangers. She'd collar people in queues to tell them how appalled she was, how outraged they should be, at another war, so irresponsibly engaged in, as if the men were just there for the killing, as if the world war, which she'd been through, had medals to prove it, could so easily be forgotten. She was accused of betrayal, but would have brought a few round. When it was all over, she told me, she stood in Hyde Park and watched the victory planes roar overhead, heard the searing whine she hoped she'd never hear again, the sound that marked her wartime dreams of my father's death, and poisoned her, I think.

Not long ago I went to the cemetery where my mother was cremated; also Nana and my grandfather, and aunt Vera; and my father too. As I walked past the rows of headstones I thought of my mother, how her ashes had been scattered there almost thirty years ago, how we had arranged for a rosebush to be planted in her memory, also for a notice in a commemorative book which would be displayed every year on the anniversary of her death, but only for seven years. We could have paid for an extension, but we hadn't, and none of us had ever set eyes on the notice, or the bush, and now, all these years later, it wasn't my mother who brought me to the cemetery but Peggy, the grandmother we'd never known and from whose premature death so much followed on.

She first appears in the official records on 5 September 1917, when, in Bradfield, then in Oxfordshire, as the daughter of Samuel Morrison, she became the wife of John Todd. She was 24; he, 38. The births in Epping and in London of their two daughters are indexed, as is Peggy's death on 9 February 1920, but we've found no record of her birth in Ireland or anywhere else, nor any other trace of her. It's as if she didn't exist before her marriage and lived to give birth to her daughters. Hers was a life memorialised only in her husband's unspoken thoughts.

I found her grave. It was overgrown, and to read the headstone I had to tear off a tangled mass of vegetation. The burial plot was a double one, as if the grieving widower had planned to join his adored young wife in eternity, a wish Nana had honoured. The second grave was empty but a stone urn, propped against the headstone, contained my grandfather's ashes.

Dear Lin, thank you for your vivid letter. I have an exhibition opening in two weeks; and this house has been sold, so I'm looking for somewhere to live/work in London. I feel I've been sleep-walking these past years, in a positive and necessary direction, but oblivious to the passage of time. I still feel adolescent and immortal, though already one-third grey-haired. Hope we meet. Victor.

Finally we did meet, at an exhibition of images of love. We sat on a bench looking at the "ill-favoured" couples of Stanley Spencer, and recognised some possibility for ourselves in their blissful domestic intimacy. They stood naked, toasting bread at a gas fire, which illuminated the man's genitals and the woman's flame of red pubic hair; or they sat side by side on a pair of lavatories, pants round their ankles like children, and she peered at his splendid erection. Most famously they lay on a tiger-skin rug, staring into one another's eyes, the animal's head between theirs, a squashed and astonished witness to a devotion that was ridiculous and yet true. These couples might be awkward and odd, even ugly, with their bellies and pitted, crepe-like skin, but they'd found love against all expectations and revelled in their good fortune.

I remember exactly the moment I made the leap of faith to commit myself to Victor. A grim November Sunday, and we had just parted to go back to our work. It had been a vexed meeting because Victor had begun to feel our love as a trap and wanted to delay our plan to live together and possibly, it seemed to me, put it off altogether. I went into the tube and through the turnstile, and as I stepped on to the escalator it came to me that Victor was my life's love and I was his, whatever his shortcomings or mine, and if I trusted that knowledge, and stayed steady and sure, what I believed in would surely transpire.

AMERICA

I decided to visit my aunt Marion in America. Hugo, who was a favourite of Marion's, encouraged me. He described her as "sweet" and "sad". I said that even someone who loved her would not call her "sweet". Nor would they find her sad. But he insisted: he'd often felt her warmth, her poignancy. Hadn't I? It's true I had nothing to complain of, she'd never been anything but generous to me. So if not sweet or sad, he asked, what was she? I couldn't answer. A few adjectives came into my head—contentious, overbearing—but I couldn't cite any particular incidents, or if I could they sounded lame. Marion had a difficult reputation, and it was as if it had been so for such a long time that I took it for granted and had forgotten what it amounted to.

The weather was said to be mild for February, with only the occasional flurry of snow, but still it was cold. I noticed the garden door was open, and aunt Marion caught my glance. "My visitors never stay long," she said. "It's too fresh for them." She laughed, and I laughed too, and felt my face stick, frozen in a grin. She had always made a point of being amusing, but I wasn't fooled—two minutes into my visit and she was serving me notice.

As she prepared a celebratory lunch I sat huddled on the couch looking at the artefacts of her English childhood.

Portraits of her mother and father, photographs of an uncle who drove carriage horses for sport, a framed certificate of the freedom of the City of London presented to her father, pieces of old-looking furniture, ornaments—"loot" was what her sisters had called all this, what they saw as Marion's booty, sequestered over the years from the family home.

We ate the lobster rolls and drank the champagne. The talk was desultory. I felt a curious disjuncture between the forms of celebration, carefully adhered to, and the actuality of a glum family meeting. Marion didn't ask much, as if she wasn't very interested, as if her declared feelings of delight at my coming were only superficial. She's old, I said to myself, her sisters are dead, and England, the English relations, don't hold out much interest for her anymore. It only later occurred to me that she didn't ask questions because she didn't want to answer any, the questions I had crossed the Atlantic to ask, questions I could no longer formulate except crassly: how had it been for her in childhood? What was her version of events? Had she been as unhappy as her sisters? Suddenly it seemed tasteless to question her—it was no business of mine.

She came up with some school stories, the usual tale of cold-water baths—in explanation of her bare feet, which she didn't cover even when she stepped out into the yard to call the cat. This was a Marion unfamiliar to me—bare feet, leggings, a sloppy sweater. She had always been famous among her English relations for her chic; symbol, with her three perfectly beautiful daughters, of the American dream.

After lunch we drove round the town. Marion told me some local gossip in between pointing out the picturesque clapboard houses. A fire had blighted one of them. The girlfriend of a friend's son had a fireman brother who'd been called out. She knew the people but hadn't phoned to offer them hospitality: "They've got lots of friends with more space than I have." The town was like a suburb, quiet and empty. There didn't seem to be a centre, where people filled the streets.

111

She dropped me off at my lodgings. Another clapboard house, and cold. I got under the blankets and wondered at the chill that gripped me.

In the morning, when she opened the door to me, I saw that she had softened—something had smoothed the lines on her face—as if she had thought better of her intransigence, and certain things could be said.

I asked about her leaving England. Hadn't it felt like a liberation? From the family, I implied, from constraints that would be released in a new country. That wasn't how she saw it. She had nothing to free herself from, it was just that she met a man she wanted to marry, and he happened to be an American.

I asked what it meant to her that her sisters and she had different mothers, and she said she hadn't known until someone at school told her that Vera and Beatrice were her half-sisters, that her mother wasn't theirs. She was 11, and nothing had ever been said. Her parents didn't want her to claim any special privileges, she explained, as if she'd never been taxed with her sisters' view of it, that on the contrary she'd been showered with privileges, that she was the favoured child. She said her first thought had been that at last she knew the identity of the woman in the photograph that always hung strangely unremarked in her sisters' room.

Then, out of nowhere, came a question from long ago: "Whatever happened to my Dresden lady?"

Once again she didn't seem to want an answer, as if it was enough to register her claim. Her husband Sam had bought her some other kind of figure in its place. "He knew Vera would never give up my lady."

Finally, she told me a story.

She remembered whiteness—white walls, white carpet, white cover on a huge double bed, and floating white curtains at a door ajar on what promised to be a balcony. Running across this white room, getting tangled in the gauzy hangings, but then she was out in the open air—sky and the tops of trees—and jumping up to lean over the wrought-iron railing. She looked down at miniature cars and people, surprised at how high she was above the street. A cab drew up, and a woman got out, looking up, not at Marion, but at a window below and along. Marion leant a little further, feeling the railing cutting into her hips, and saw the woman wave before paying off the taxi.

Then, a hand on her back, followed by a fierce tug at her skirt pulling her off the rail. She toppled when she landed, fell backwards, and looked up at her sisters: Vera pale and blank-faced, and Beatrice with that trembling look, about to dissolve into laughter or tears, one never knew which.

Vera, getting her colour back, shrugged, and then the friend they were visiting came out on the balcony and said, "So you found our view," and prattled on, like an estate agent Vera would say in the car going home.

"What happened?" I asked.

"One of them pulled me off the railing, but it's only now occurred to me that the other was about to push me over."

"Which one?"

But Marion just shrugged.

ALL THIS

I wondered why it felt as if I'd been there before. Then I remembered the holiday house in Dorset we went to when we were very young children. It was the trees. Four tall trees that stood along the side of the lane opposite my father's cottage, just as at the Dorset house. Of course I thought that was why he chose it—because it reminded him of a past happiness, those summers in Dorset—but he denied it. He said he couldn't remember the trees as I did; the way they thrashed about in the wind, threatening to crash down on the roof of the house and smash us all to smithereens. "It's quite different here," he said, as if to reassure me.

There's a photo somewhere of Simon at that house in Dorset. He wears a girl's swimsuit, with a bib, like boys did then, and he's standing in the middle of a lawn with a flower-bed and an old wall behind him. He's grimacing ecstatically as my father points a water hose at him. You can't see my father, only his tensed hands grasping the hose, and what can be read into them? A touch of cruelty?—in his determination to finish the business of dowsing his son with ice-cold water.

My father didn't consult us about moving but simply announced the fact one evening when we were assembled at the house for supper. Hugo, at his most pompous, wondered if

114

he wasn't acting rashly. Better, he advised, to wait a year before making any life decisions. My father pounced on that.

"Life decisions!" he jeered. "This isn't a life decision. I'm preparing for death."

"Exactly." Hugo turned harsh—and looked to me for confirmation; all I could think of was, "But you've always loved London."

"And now I'm returning, as old men should, to my roots. The Black Country."

I'd been made to understand that I'd be coming to an idyllic spot, the perfect place to finish my convalescence. He showed me round proudly, especially the garden, which was given over to vegetables. He picked up a fistful of earth and explained how he'd sifted all the stones out of it, and then he looked at me and laughed as if in answer to my incomprehension.

Home-grown vegetables had taken on a mystical dimension for my father. Digging them up was a ritual, conducted twice a day—at midday, after returning from his morning walk, and at 5.30, before supper. He cleaned and cooked them meticulously and then ate as if he were running late for his next appointment, stuffing carrots and potatoes into his mouth, apparently swallowing them whole. Followed by tea and cake.

The kitchen was the best room. Every morning I was glad to reach it, across the dim living-room, empty except for the television and two upright chairs. It was like a lean-to against the back of the house, a sloping roof and then mostly window— and it was often sunny in the mornings, when I took possession. "All yours," my father would say as he set out on his walk. Six or seven miles a day, so he was fitter, he said, than he'd ever been.

Every morning I drank my tea from my mother's breakfast cup, bought in a market in the south of France, and just one of the things she collected, that stood about the family house, objects I could list as in a game of Pelmanism: the china dog, the barometer in an elephant tusk, the chipped papier-mâché box, the bowl made of shells, the cut-glass decanter … "We'll need a bulldozer," my father said, "to remove them." They annoyed him, all her things, all those years. He felt relieved to be able to pack all her clutter away at last.

"So you won't be giving me a granddaughter," my father said soon after I arrived, referring to the recent operation to remove my womb. A statement that turned into a question, as if as an afterthought, like twisting the knife—as if it wasn't too late, and I could still, if I tried, did my utmost, give him what he wanted. Simon would know about that, who despaired of ever meeting our father's eye, let alone his expectations. "I'd have liked a granddaughter, a little girl." And he stuffed a cake into his mouth, all of it, in one voracious bite.

I leant forward, my palms flat on the table to keep myself calm. "I can't picture a girl," I said. "If I'd had one, though, I'd have called her Siena."

"Ah—Victor's favourite city."

My last but one morning. The cup seemed even more chipped than before, so I had to place my lips carefully. I said as much to the boy, who played at my feet. Intent, he didn't look up at me, just grunted. He didn't have a name, the boy. Can a phantom have a name? Perhaps he was his father, Victor, in his childlike aspect, that which I nurtured and comforted. He had silky hair, which I liked to touch, cupping his head in my hands and looking deep into his moist, tender eyes.

The boy had got hold of a bag of wood blocks and was building a house with them. He said it was a tower, but the fourth level of bricks was askew. There … it toppled, and he sighed, rueful. Make a wider base, I suggested, and taper the sides as it gets higher, like a pyramid. The boy rejected my suggestion. He didn't want a pyramid but a tower, straight sides, up to

116

the sky. The determination to realise the initial conception. No compromises. Persistent, he held on to his idea, stubborn as a bull.

The sun was lost behind clouds and I felt chilled. I reached to light a burner on the stove. Then I sat back comfortably, drawing my dressing-gown over my knees. I wore a sweater too, over the gown, and I was tempted to stay like that all morning, cocooned in my corner by the burner, comforted by its hiss, which drowned the whispering sounds that came when the wind was up; staring out of the window and thinking of this and that. Suddenly my view was filled by the round face of a youth pressed flat against the glass of the window. He saw me cowering in my corner, and was gone. George. "My right-hand man," was how my father referred to him.

I saw them in the garden from my window when I went up to dress. They were bending over the vegetable runnels, and I feared for my father's back. It didn't seem to trouble him like it once had, but he was still the clumsiest of men with a spade. George took over and began digging with a grace that was a joy to watch—and my father looked on admiringly. Then he grasped his shoulder and George smiled, half shy, half proud. My father walked across the turfy lawn towards the cottage, disappearing through the back door beneath me, not looking up though I had an idea he'd seen me, from the rigid set of his head, and the studied way he kept his eyes looking straight ahead.

As I came down the stairs I heard George's high, tuneless whistle above the sound of water splashing into the kitchen sink. I had to brace myself before going in to join them. My father was scrubbing mud off carrots while George, at the table, cut slices from a block of cheese. They weren't talking, but there was an intimacy in their silence, as if they stood like that, side by side, preparing food, every day of their lives.

I waited a moment too long before crossing the threshold, so that I felt awkward, an intruder in their privacy.

117

My awkwardness made me clumsy, and I knocked the door against the corner of the dresser. They both jumped and looked round in surprise.

George dropped the knife on to the table with a clang that drowned my hello. I asked if I could help with lunch, and my father, in a breezy voice, suggested I sit down. "Too many cooks …" he said as he put the vegetables on to boil, adding salt with a flick of his fingers. "Move along a bit, George," who was blocking my way. "Let Lin sit down." George moved along, turning his back on me and staring out of the window as he ate his sandwich.

His silence discomfited me. It made me talk louder, insensitively. I could hear the false notes in the pitch of my voice—like my mother's. It was disconcerting how often I recognised my mother in me, almost thought I was her. It was as if I'd wanted her to survive in me but didn't altogether like the result. Nor did George.

I asked questions. First, how was my father's walk? Bracing, as usual. And then, at George's masticating jaw, how was the wall?—his masterwork, the rebuilding of my father's wall, no more than a pile of rubble when he moved in. I could see from his jaw that George had stopped chewing, but he didn't turn towards me, and his answer was a crumbly grunt. Leaving my father to enthuse. "Almost there, I'd say. A couple of feet to go, eh, George?"

One last, great swallow and then, "I'll be off." Head down he made for the back door.

My father put a plate of vegetables in front of me. "Straight from the soil," he said. "Do you the world of good." Then he asked me to shop for supper on my walk to the village. "You are going, aren't you?" he said. "As usual?"

"Yes, I'll go. One more time. What else shall I buy? For our last dinner. Sardines, baked beans, frozen peas, Cadbury's Whole Nut …?"

"Baked beans and chocolate," said my father. "We'll have a feast." He looked me in the eye and smiled. Was there any smile sweeter than his? It lit up his face, gave it flesh and roundness—and it dissolved my resistance.

The light from the television screen attracted a moth which made a blemish on the newsreader's neck. I expected her to brush it off, a little fantasy that distracted me from what she was saying. Not my father. He watched television with the utmost concentration. If I said something he grunted in reply as if to say, not now, I want to listen.

Abruptly the newsreader changed tack. We watched an MP newly elected in a by-election beam triumphantly at his cheering supporters. He was flanked by his wife, who kissed him full on the lips (the moth zoomed off), and two children. The little girl smiled engagingly, but her older brother looked sullen, as if he hoped his connection with the victorious family would be overlooked. He stood to one side; and then we saw him dodge behind a man who tried to put an arm round him to draw him into the family circle. The camera hastily shifted from this awkwardness to focus instead on the happy couple whose smiles, however, began to look fixed.

The boy reminded me of Simon who, lest we forget him in his no-man's-land between my father and me and my mother and Hugo, was forced to make his presence felt by his absence in a place as far away as he could get.

My father switched off the television and I waited in the darkness while he felt his way to turn on the light switch. He looked cadaverous, then, all bone and harsh shadows.

While he was in the bathroom I opened the front door and stared at the blackness. Then I stepped out and closed the door behind me. I edged my way down the path and felt for the gate. The trees along the opposite side of the lane made a sound like a deep sigh of relief, but then, as I was about to set

119

off, I heard a squeal, high and piercing. I turned and started back up the path until I remembered, of course, the pigs at the farm down the road. I let myself into the cottage, thinking of Victor, hearing myself tell him, laughing, about my fear, pooh-poohing his concern at my walking alone at night.

I wasn't asleep when the storm started, or not properly, but in a half-sleep, so that nothing was quite real or as it should be. I was surrounded by noise, the thunder and thrashing trees and the rain hitting the roof, and I knew I should get up and close the window, but it seemed impossible to get out of bed. The only thing to do was to stay where I was, hunched up under the blankets.

Then I became convinced that the boy, my child, was out in the storm. I saw him all alone under a tree, hugging the tree because that was all he had to give him comfort. He was weeping in terrible distress, and I was powerless to help him, to soothe him or lead him to shelter. I was too far away, it seemed, hundreds and thousands of miles or years away, and incapable of crossing the wide, black void that separated us …

… and now, so many years later, when all this is a distant memory, I'm looking out for Victor. He comes into view, a white hulk like a bear, struggling across the snow-bound square towards me. My heart leaps and I limp to the front door. Without a coat or changing my shoes, I seize my stick and step out, gingerly making my way towards him. Then we're like two bears, lumbering stickily towards one another, and when we meet we're both laughing. I clutch at him and we slip and slide. He yells at me to desist, and we just manage to save ourselves. As we slowly, arm in arm, cross the road to the house I point out my footprints, already disappearing beneath another layer of snow.

PART THREE

THE GOOD DOCTOR

PIGEON

Did a noise wake me? Or was it that I woke and then heard a noise? Or even dreamt of a noise and woke? I listened for the sound to repeat itself. I was always—still am—nervously, hysterically, alert to the possibility of mice. I think I see them at the periphery of my vision, darting along the skirting board, disappearing somewhere. Or hear them, almost worse, the scratching sound unseen that is unmistakably them. The words that come to mind: invasive, out of control. But this was different. The soft flap of wings and an insistent tap. I sat up and switched on the light to see that the clock showed three a.m. and that a pigeon was sitting comfortably on my table. There was no question of my bearing it. I struggled to get out of bed and then staggered and stumbled towards the door, my feet sticking to the floor, risking a fall in my rush to leave the room. I called Victor's name as I descended the stairs and he woke. He told me to get into bed with him, that we'd deal with it in the morning—an unacceptable strategy to me, envisaging as I did pigeon shit all over my room. So Victor got out of bed and went to look. He called down to me, "There's no pigeon. You're imagining it," and when I went up again I saw the truth of it. The "pigeon" was a floppy cloth bag, faintly grey, faintly pigeon-like. Victor pointed out that the window was open a crack—not nearly enough to allow a

123

pigeon in. He was sour—"So now you've added pigeons to your list of fears. You're such a fearful person, not a day goes by without my being reminded of it. Your fear is your cross—and mine," he said.

I retaliated: "How would you like a pigeon in your room? I can't see your liking it any more than I do."

"But you haven't got a pigeon in your room."

THE GOOD DOCTOR

That's how our friend referred to him. "The good doctor"—without irony, I think. He'd been seeing him for years; a fine person, he said, perceptive, sensitive, clever. My first thought was that this might be someone who could throw light on my myriad fears. Victor had the same idea: "It sounds as if you've found your man."

The pigeon was the catalyst. I hadn't in fact been looking for anyone, man or woman, but my anxieties were becoming ever more entrenched, which may have been a sign that trouble lay ahead—and Victor too had a sense of it. What had begun as an inquiry into my illness, what it meant for me, had turned into a remembering of my childhood, which seemed to expose vulnerabilities I had no idea how to resolve. My brother Hugo warned me against delving into my psyche so late in life. "Don't stir the shit," he said, but I believed that that was exactly what I had to do.

On the phone, making an arrangement to meet, and then remaking it, the good doctor twice called me Jane, and when he opened the door and greeted me he put a slight emphasis on my name, *Lin*, as if to say he'd get it right from now on.

With a practised manner he directed me upstairs to a small room at the top of the house. Papered in a dark green, it felt enclosing, warmly so on that first occasion, but later,

125

sometimes, constraining, despite the wide-open sky beyond the window. The doctor sat at a desk, and I took the other chair. There was also a couch, with which I would have an uneasy relationship. Every so often I would lie on it in hope of talking freely; failing, I would abandon it for the chair and regard it with dismay, a reproach to my inhibitions.

"What can I do for you?"

I liked his directness, and was charmed by his sweetness of mien, and I replied that I felt anxious about many things, despite my life of loving harmony with Victor, work that I enjoyed, and loyal friends. Not just bombs and plane crashes but mice, and birds, and sheep that barred my way in fields, and strangers at parties. I identified with ill-treated donkeys and horses sacrificed to war; and the slightest misfortune suffered by child or beast would move me to tears. Sometimes, too, I felt overwhelmed by feelings of presentiment and, as if with some special insight into the future, I anticipated imminent disaster. I mentioned my illness, what it meant for me, how I thought I could best live with it. He heard me out and asked a few questions about my family. I described the parental drama that had dominated my childhood and youth—torn between my father's devotion to me and my mother's jealousy, and my love for both—and he objected to my theorised presentation of our three-way relations. I don't think I named Oedipus but he did and found its application pat. "People have feelings," he said, not for the last time. He would often ask: "But what did you *feel*?" after I'd given an account of something. He believed feeling memories were a more accurate guide to a person's past than visual memories, which were easily embroidered by wishful thinking or revenge. It was a constant refrain with him that I failed to talk about my feelings, or rather, if I talked about them, I did so with a cerebral detachment. I didn't feel my feelings, express them, in his presence.

He concluded: "I think I can help you."

126

IN LOVE

Not a phrase the good doctor liked; a condition that in his view had little to do with love. ("How can you love someone you don't know?") For him it was just "brainstem stuff". But it served, it seemed to me, to denote the surge of feeling that may be largely transferred from the pattern established by a childhood relationship but is no less overwhelming for that.

My penchant as a young woman for men who weren't free or drawn to reciprocate my fancy hadn't troubled me in the thirty years since meeting Victor. Somehow, with him, my feelings bypassed the fault-line that had often engulfed me before, and in our first years together it seemed that nothing less than a miracle had enabled me to leave behind my habit of unrequited love. I remember the happiness of that time, how we relished our life together in a tiny flat in the centre of town. We worked hard and enjoyed our friends and travelled. We were privileged but after our difficult twenties felt we deserved our pleasures. In the first year there were conflicts as we found a way of living together (more than once Victor walked out into the night after an argument neither of us could recall a few days later), and I was shy, fearful, unsociable, and floundering in an art milieu that made demands I felt I couldn't meet. And there were setbacks. Our childlessness was a disappointment, though, having found Victor, I felt it was greedy to want a child as well, as if two miracles were too many to ask for. My fault-line was mostly far from my conscious mind but I knew it lay waiting to drag me again into the mire if my circumstances changed. Victor was my protection, and as long as we remained together I believed I'd be safe. The trigger for a repetition—or perhaps a regression—so many years later was partly the good doctor, his fatherly role (though he wasn't many years older than me), his attractiveness, and his expectation that I open my mind for his inspection; and partly a drug I'd begun to take, that had the unwanted side-effect of heightening my libido, interacting with my psyche to home in on the fault-line, and making the doctor the object of my passion.

In the beginning my lust had no sentimental aspect; the banality of the scenes I fantasised of mutual passion and ecstasy should have alerted me to its essential falseness. Contained by the small, featureless space in which I envisaged the act's exploding, it was there and then gone, so that when I next encountered the doctor my sex thoughts were absent—until a second visitation, and then we were children at play, the doctor and me, fondling one another, with smutty jokes; it was fun, illicit, but also innocent.

When I confessed my desire to him he wanted to know what form my fantasy took, and I was unable to find the words to describe it—not because I couldn't find the right words, or there wasn't a vocabulary, but because I had no words at all. Suddenly I was without language, just a mass of desolate, incomprehensible feeling.

SEDUCTION

I happened to see a film that for me evoked the atmosphere of the early sessions with the doctor. Set in France at the end of the war, it tells of how a woman, a communist and an atheist, widow of a member of the resistance, challenges the religious convictions of the village priest. He lends her books in hope of drawing her back into the church. A dialogue develops between them, and friendship follows. Then "a catastrophe occurs": she recovers her faith (we're referred to Jeremiah 20:7: "The lord has seduced me and I have allowed myself to be seduced"). The priest appears erotically in her dreams. When, one day, she touches his hand, he violently pulls it away and flees, and she doesn't see him again for several months. He may or may not be aware of her emotional engagement with him, he may or may not be aware of his own with her, but his adherence to the rule of chastity is absolute—and the abstinence required by his vocation allows him to enjoy the company of his parishioner without entanglement. So it seemed with the doctor. He deployed his exceptional gift for intimacy, with appreciative glances, suggestive stares, and softly modulated voice, to secure my feelings for the benefit of the treatment—with a certain carelessness, it seemed to me, given my history of loving where love wouldn't be returned.

"Say whatever is in your mind but never touch." The doctor repeated this homily many times. "One mustn't act out one's feelings." "We—you and I—don't touch." I came to think he addressed these warnings to himself as much as to me. But though I desired him passionately I knew I'd fail to respond to any amorousness on his part, and I took to keeping my coat on to discourage his stares.

One day, I told him about my love for Victor. I regretted that I'd done so, or wished I hadn't felt I had to. I feared he'd take it to heart, think I meant it—which I did as well as not meaning it, because never in my right mind did I forget my reality. But I seemed also to possess a parallel consciousness in which I cast aside all prior loyalties, even in love, even to Victor. With my mind's eye I envisaged the doctor subsumed by a red cloud, a sexual being, his interest focused on me. Sometimes my father appeared, by contrast, thin, pale, severe, and exactly delineated, the Apollonian to the doctor's Dionysian. It seemed that it was as the doctor said, I separated desire and love, and simply and directly split my conflicted feelings for my father between him and the doctor.

I came to think that a psychic confluence involving us both marked the early months of the therapy. I found the doctor transparent. It was as if I knew his mind and could intuit the sense behind hints he dropped about his life. For me this endowed the relationship with the potential for perfect happiness, a state of bliss I believed I'd had a promise of at a very young age and had then been denied. Now I know that my disappointment will never be assuaged, nor will speaking of it ever resolve it.

THRESHOLDS

"Sooner or later, you're going to have to get up": walking across the square with Victor, on our way to get a coffee, I trip on a raised paving stone and find myself sprawling face down on the ground and weeping. Not a serious fall—I weep not from pain but from frustration and self-pity, like a child who is inconsolable because she has dropped her ice-cream cone. Also from the uncertainty of life, that a momentary wrong footing can undermine a person's fundamental sense of wellbeing, or even kill them. And perhaps too because I always hope that I won't fall again, that finally I've learnt my lesson and found out how not to fall, and so long as I don't fall the illness won't get worse, a sort of touching wood.

I fell on the beach once, at the village we go to in Devon. As I ran down the pebbled slope towards the sea, I went faster and faster and took smaller and smaller steps until I was on tiptoe and suddenly I froze and while my feet stayed fixed to the ground momentum took my body forward and I fell headlong. Festination: Latin *festinare*, to hasten. Adding a classical gloss is somehow a comfort. I feel virtuous, intellectually alive—no descent into self-pity for me. Even the simple act of taking the heavy dictionary off the shelf is calming and counteracts any tendency to haste or panic. "Drop your heels," I command myself as my feet begin to festinate. "Flatten your toes. Make your feet equal to the task of carrying you." I take care not to turn abruptly and to go through barriers and doorways mindfully.

Someone told me that freezing is a threshold problem, psychologically speaking, and it's easy to list the possible associations: reluctance to move forward into the next stage of life, or to engage with a new experience, wanting only to stay safely where one is. I found it difficult to leave home, expecting disaster either in the flat while I was gone; or perhaps for myself while I was out.

Victor is steady, matter-of-fact, always my mainstay. I take hold of his outstretched hand and let him pull me to my feet. Generally I land on my knees; with impaired reflexes I fail to put out my hand to soften my fall. But better knees that are bruised and knobbly than a fractured wrist or finger.

SHAME

The doctor called me, variously, "just" a middle-class lady, a conformist, and a careerist more interested in publishing my stories than writing them; also a miserly type. All these tags were bound to annoy me. I thought he'd got me wrong and was either peculiarly unperceptive or perhaps even muddling me with someone else. I couldn't immediately find the words to refute him, and when I later complained he asked why I couldn't respond in the moment, instead of dwelling for a week on what he'd said, letting it fester. I objected too to his picture of my sitting silently at dinner parties and thinking how stupid everyone was (how could I when I was consumed by shame?). I told him about Tom's birthday dinner. At what point did the rot set in? I was open and relaxed when we arrived. Tom's son was unrecognisable with his new punk's haircut, and I introduced myself as if I didn't know him. "I'm Charlie," he said. "God! So you are," I replied, and there was laughter. But by the time we were at dinner I'd lost my way. It's like a performance, and I can't sustain it, I haven't the stamina, or perhaps the belief, and once the silence sets in I can't break it. What are the conditions? Nerves make me stupid and ashamed. I fear being snubbed and not standing up for myself. At one point, for example, Tom queried the existence of a book I referred to and, rather than insist, I immediately

133

backed down. But I was right, it existed, and later I found it on a shelf at home.

The doctor's view: generally it doesn't matter if you go to a party or not, and if you don't think about it in advance, if you don't let it become a moral issue when it's a matter of convention, you might find yourself deciding to go. He also said that if I wanted I could become a live wire in my old age—but why would I want that? I'd like to be more fully and more honestly myself, not a false persona with a hollow core.

"But what would that be?" he asked. "Being 'honestly yourself'. From conception onwards outside influences shape a person's character and fate."

"What I mean is that though a person is constructed—by herself, and by her parents and teachers and friends, as well as by experiences and chance and fortune and fate—in spite of this she can tell her story, including the story of her construction, consistently and in a way that seems true. I want to be able to do that."

After several months on the couch I was sitting on the chair because of my bad back (which he seemed to disbelieve). He commented on my black clothes, which he also seemed to suspect ("Are you sad?"). I was wearing a skirt for the first time in months, out of a sort of seductiveness, to test him, but he didn't look at my knees. I was in an edgy mood. He said: "Do I detect a certain irritation?" I apologised for being grumpy. He said, "Don't apologise. You're lucky to be free to be grumpy. *I'm not.*" Later I realised my mood, which was unfamiliar, may have had something to do with its being the anniversary of my mother's death. That night I dreamed of rats and mice swarming in a closed room.

GRIEF

In Rome with Victor for the first Christmas after starting sessions with the doctor, I felt a yearning for him alternately with grief for my mother, dead some thirty years but still the object of my love and guilt. I recalled a recent episode with a dog: tied up outside the supermarket, it barked with the desperation of a creature abandoned. I offered it comfort, distraction, but it hardly drew breath before resuming its howling. As I retreated I thought of my mother, a dog-lover, and found myself struggling to hold back my tears. She came to mind too in the early morning, when I often woke myself with a shouted injunction like "Don't do it!" "Help!" "Get out!" And the tears would spill over. Left to themselves, my sobs would erupt in a wail, but I'd think of Victor and the sleeping neighbours all round and fix my face in what felt like a mask of mourning, my mouth wide open, lips pulled back from my teeth as if I was snarling, and I'd emit only a strangled whine. I was stricken by grief—that's what it amounted to—but why? Did I cry for my mother? For myself?

At the best of times Victor and I disturb each other at night. I wake to his snores, or he to my sleep talk. He hears voices, different voices, mine and others', all channelled through me in sleep. Unintelligible sounds with the tone and rhythms of

135

language, interspersed, he says, with what he calls chortling. "I'm glad about the laughter," I said, the first time, and he was particular: "Not laughter, *chortling*." I've heard these voices only once, in a half-sleep, when they seemed at first to come from across the room but then shifted and were within me and I could silence them. In a dream I envisaged a hieroglyphic text that represented what they said, but it meant nothing to me. I'm told my brain is playing tricks, mention is made of crossed neuronal pathways; the drugs are held responsible, or the illness itself, but neither explains what feels like a shadow cast by the circumstances of my childhood long ago.

In the middle of our first night in Rome, unable to sleep, I moved from the bedroom to another room in the flat we'd rented. As I felt my way from the bed to the door I had the impression there were three of us in the room, Victor and me, and one other. I turned to look and saw no one, but though I was imagining it my sense of it was as somehow true. Was my mind conjuring the doctor as the third of our trio? Or rather, had I conjured my father? Or my mother, come to that?

I lay on an unmade bed in a waking dream. I was the doctor's daughter, or not quite, more an appendage to his daughter. We'd lost him and tramped the streets in search of him but never found him. Then, still half asleep, I imagine I'm sitting at a table in the doctor's hallway along with other people: a party. A daughter comes in and greets him. I'm aware that behind me they're embracing. They're quite still, and remain locked in each other's arms for a long time. I glance behind me and he's bent low over her and I can't see his face. There's a desperate longing in his embrace while she is accepting but doesn't reciprocate, tolerant of his great need but allowing a certain reserve to mark her response.

One morning in Rome, Victor came to find me and we made love so sweetly that I wept at the poignancy of it. But he complained I was a glum companion. He objected when I rang the doctor (who, no less at a loss, suggested I try to enjoy

136

my holiday), and would for some time continue to make jokes about my infatuation. I found myself going along with it, laughing with him, and playing down the intensity of my feelings. It was galling but salutary when I resumed after the Christmas break to find that the doctor, who looked dishevelled and as if in some kind of crisis, had forgotten my name and almost everything about me.

A week later he had done his homework. He greeted me warmly, and opened the conversation rather than leaving me to initiate it. He had read a story of mine and was appreciative, complimentary even. My notebook doesn't record the detail and I can't remember the substance of his comments. But then, a week or so after that, it was as if nothing I said was right. He complained that I spoke in headlines, when he wanted the detail. But no, he didn't want me to "do" anything (no "shoulds") and urged me to talk of my feelings. Wasn't that what I was doing? It was often like that: a session in which he showered me with praise would be followed by one of scoldings and criticism.

I was always nervous before sessions. Wanting not to appear stupid or trivial, wanting instead the doctor's approval, fearful of his contempt and his anger. Arriving early, I would walk in the park and try to sort out in my mind what to say and how to say it, reluctant to let this happen spontaneously as I was supposed to. I liked to have an agenda to start me off. In theory it would lead to other, unpremeditated subjects of a revelatory kind. Usually it didn't, and then I was only too likely to resort to small talk, cultural chit-chat about exhibitions, and so on. He was generous in sharing anecdotes from his life that I certainly didn't need to know, but he refused ever to be drawn on his feelings about me, good or bad.

THREESOME

On the tube one day, I saw a little girl sitting on her father's lap. Kissing and stroking his cheek, whispering in his ear, she was all over him, and turned her back on her mother when she addressed them from across the aisle. The father responded kindly to the child, also to her mother, who remained steadfast in the face of her young daughter's display of rivalry, took her hand quite naturally when they got up to leave the train.

The doctor laughed wryly at my account and asked for an association. What came to mind was a winter evening after tea, in the Hampstead house. I was loitering in the hall with my younger brother Simon. The drawing-room door was ajar and we could hear our parents talking. I don't think we were eavesdropping exactly—Simon sat astride a tricycle, and I watched him—but we both overheard my mother's complaint: "You make such a fuss of Lin." And my father's protesting reply: "What's wrong with that? She's my daughter." Simon laughed in an exaggerated way, and I joined in, knowing that I also sounded false as I tried to disguise my feelings of shame. Shame and guilt. It was as if I'd been caught out by my mother in an ugly act. I didn't know what that act could possibly be, but clearly I had hurt her.

When, now, I try to recall what may have preceded that exchange, I can dimly picture myself sitting on my father's knee, at the centre of his attention. I may have been five or six—it's possible that what I'm remembering here is an early memory rather than the scene itself. My brothers are present as well as my mother; perhaps we're having tea in front of the drawing-room fire. I don't have any particular feeling about it. I was on my father's lap, that's all, and, a man of warm feeling, he was stroking my cheek and teasing me.

A dream, mine. We're walking, the doctor and I, side by side towards the park. We know we mustn't touch but as we swing our arms, my left and his right, our hands brush one against the other, and I feel the flutter of his fingers against mine. I want nothing so much as to grasp his hand, to grasp him. My desire is great but so also is the penalty for touching and I have to restrain myself. I notice that we're both stark naked, which seems to be acceptable—though touching is not. Images came to mind of the expulsion of Adam and Eve. Was it then, or at some other time, that I bought for the doctor a selection of exotic fruits from a greengrocer called The Garden of Eden? I did this without consciousness of the implications, which the doctor pointed out to me.

In a story I wrote after my father's death I moved him to the flat, scrubby countryside of his native Black Country. I invented a helping hand for him, an awkward and silent young man called George. On a visit one day, the "I" who's telling the story walks into the kitchen and sees them through the open door of the bathroom beyond. The father has his bare back towards her, and George, with a bottle of antiseptic in one hand, dabs at his shoulders, which are criss-crossed with a mass of cuts. Her first thought is: he's had an accident, fallen into bramble or barbed wire; but then she sees that these aren't jagged scratches but neat, deliberate little cuts. It occurs to her that they are no accident, the cuts, but something that George does to her father, that her father asks him to do.

This is nothing short of melodrama, but though it has little to do with my father, this scene suggests I wanted him to be punished—for what reason I couldn't exactly say. But a friend who read it spoke about the "souring of that mother/child sweetness": "the half-conscious cruelty of the father's paying too much attention—unsettling attention—to his daughter in some class/intellect game played against his wife, and then stirring the mother against her child." And once again I felt confused, as if condemned for ever to be torn in half between them, and then there was only the good doctor who would do. He, for his part, cautioned me against thinking badly of my father. He hadn't abused me and perhaps he'd even taught me to love. It may be that the relationship had gone on too long and threatened to get out of hand, but I'd found Victor, my life's love, in the end.

I wept only once in the doctor's presence, and that was when I felt an overwhelming guilt towards my parents because of all I had condemned them for—for using me as a pawn to score off each other, apparently impervious to the effect on me; for silencing my attempts to speak of my distress; for turning passionate love into a matter of shame; but at home, at night and especially when I woke in the morning, I cried, and cried. It was as if I was discarding a huge burden of grief, a lifetime's mourning for love that had been stymied by the mute denial of feeling, by silence.

AGEING

Our nightly turn round the square: I'm thinking of dailiness, repetition, the possibility of integrity; and how the exigencies of life rub up against one another, attract or repel; whether things link up to make a whole, or are irretrievably at odds.

Victor is stargazing. He stops us at the corner and we look up at a sky that's clear and unusually black so that the evening star shines brightly.

"Stardust," he says. "We all come from stardust. It's what we're made of and what in the end our ashes will return to—luminously, eternally."

Victor wants to die in the square, where we've lived already for a quarter of a century. I like to imagine how he'll be, an old man on his own. He'll turn the flat into a series of studios for painting and writing, with beds here and there. He'll lie on mine and talk out loud to me, as they say the bereaved do. I won't be here or anywhere. I won't even know I'm nowhere. I'll be dead. But Victor will be living his life, not noticing the half-eaten meals, plates with rancid remains sticking to them, the glasses smeary with fingerprints and dried-up red wine, in the way of old men. He'll have his work, his paintings and his books, and they'll be a comfort to him, as will his young friends, and all the more so in the flat he lived in with me for so many years.

141

For now we're sitting, on high stools, at a local Italian bar to watch television as we drink our coffee. A woman performs one of those tuneful, heart-felt laments of the sixties, the kind that *chanteurs* like Charles Aznavour or Françoise Hardy used to sing. I don't recognise the singer, but I know the old number she's singing, a dirge for a lost love. She acts out the words with an awkward choreography involving a window and a chair, and when she's called upon to get to her feet from the chair she falters slightly as if her knees are playing up. There's character in her face, though she has tried to disguise it with makeup, and the jeans she wears make no concessions to her thickened torso. Still, her voice touches me, and when she's finished, and the young presenters of the show are laughing, I feel tears welling up; my mouth is trembling, and a sob threatens to explode. Easy to laugh at the spectacle of a woman who inhabits a life she's grown out of, but she's also plucky and game, and who's to say the words she sings are a lie?

Or perhaps, like me, she thinks of herself as a woman still in her prime: in her mid-forties, say, unworried by incipient wrinkles and greying hair, with a still lively physicality, a sharp mind, and an awareness of her charms. But I can claim none of those attributes. I'm old and ill, and it's as if I'm stuck in the moment I learnt that my malady was Parkinson's disease and affections like stiffness, slowness, and a festinating gait were declared to be the result of a deficiency in the brain and could not be cured. Was it the shock that stopped me in my tracks? Or is it that every deterioration in my state has been attributed to a sick body rather than an ageing one?—and only now does it occur to me that a new point of view is required.

It's all around us. Ageing. People losing their health, in body and mind, dying. There's a woman in the square who has my illness. I can tell by the look of her. I feel the signs as my own: *so that's what I look like*. There's a particular cast to the stiffness, the way the shoulders hunch, the knees bend, and the feet don't quite pick up, resulting in a shuffle. The face is a mask, flat, inexpressive. And then her hands—they've lost their litheness, hang on the end of her arms, nerveless, with fingers like bunches of bananas. She's bent over, her chin digging into her chest, and she sits with her carer on a bench in the gardens without moving, like statuary. She could be asleep, even though her fingers are plucking at her skirt. A pretty skirt, a paisley pattern, but it doesn't suit her. In the days, at least a decade ago, when I used to exchange neighbourly remarks with her on the pavement outside our houses, she always wore black. Perhaps, now that she isn't responsible for herself, someone is imposing an unsuitable style on her. Tall, thin, formidable, she wore clothes to match her severity. Her hair, which now falls to her shoulders in grey tails, was once black and pinned up. I wonder how much she minds the loss of style—whether she even notices.

It's not clear how much her mind is impaired. Nor mine, come to that—though I think I'm alert to my peculiarities. My memory for recent events has long been unreliable. I've become a ditherer, losing things in my bag, grappling for money in my purse, dropping and spilling things. I've demonstrated some odd behaviour: leaving home in mis-matched shoes, not recognising people I've met a few days before, generally not articulating clearly so that I'm aware of people being unsure what to make of me. Now I use a stick it's easier; they just put me down as somehow afflicted, and shop assistants help me with my purse: "Put that away, darling."

Not a lot is asked of us to show we belong on the right side of the line, the bright side. I remember today's date without difficulty; also the name of the prime minister, and my telephone number. Such knowledge is proof enough, I'm told, that my mind is in working order, though it seems to me that there will be perfectly intelligent people in the world who don't keep track of the date, or have given up on politics. Also, no one enquires about the rigidity of my thought processes, a slowness in taking in new information and responding to the implications; or about my difficulty in retaining an idea long enough to note it.

HE DISTANCES HIMSELF

At a certain point, I saw him struggling to control his stares. His eyes began to glaze and then he blinked several times and turned away to look out of the window instead of at me. That was the last of it but not of its repercussions. I became preoccupied, or better, obsessed, with my need to talk about the currents that I believed had flowed between us. I felt it was up to him to raise the matter, not me, because I wanted his affirmation of my attractiveness, I suppose, proof of his trust and esteem, even because I felt shame for colluding—did I perhaps elicit his stares? I was occasionally guilty of dressing provocatively (I dressed for him, though I suspected that my severity, like my height and angularity were not to his taste); and once or twice I spoke too frankly of sex (he was clearly disapproving of these actings out). I gave him many opportunities to refer to what I'd perceived as the sexual charge between us in our early meetings but he never responded to my cues. Sometimes he muttered things under his breath that might have been references to what had so nearly occurred (except that in fact it had been very far from occurring). There was something about the start of a love affair, as if he was comparing that to the start of therapy, a stage of initial infatuation that had to be worked through; also the tendency of certain "types" to become fond too soon and mistake, he implied, a crush for love. My deep, agonised silences came about because I was unable to pick up on these gnomic utterances and say the only words I wanted to speak. They were like the silences of the shy, anxious, stranger-phobic five-year-old I'd once been, withholding speech as the only weapon she had to make a protest. I read of elective mutism, how the anxiety of its sufferers sets off a fight or flight response so speech shuts down whenever it's required of us. What I wanted to say remained unspoken but filled my mind, leaving no space for any other thoughts. It seemed to me that, burdened though I already was with my own passionate feelings, I was being forced to take responsibility also for what the doctor had brought to our early meetings while he distanced himself with a tight little smile. This imbalance might bring insights in therapeutic terms, but it was objectionable as a paradigm for human relations, compounded a thousand times when a man had authority over a woman. He would likely say that I was enraged simply because he didn't fulfil my desire, but I felt the injustice of his denial, of the unspokenness of his feeling— hiding behind his privilege of silence.

I was slow to realise that my thoughts about the doctor had become angry ones. The despair I felt after every session, too black for me to identify its parts, would lift after a day or two and give way to rage. Sometimes I would lie in bed at night developing, so I believed, an argument that showed that the doctor had been insulting, or negligent, or contradictory. Every so often I would switch on the light and try writing down a thought (I can't write, can't hold my hand back, which starts in harness, but then takes on a life of its own and gallops like a wild horse to the edge of the page: another sort of festination). In the morning, the words would be indecipherable or, if readable, then meaningless.

NEWS FROM ELSEWHERE

Occasionally, signs of a world beyond penetrated the dense cloud of my obsession and was registered by my conscious mind. I was collecting mint from the overgrown bush out back when the phone rang. I hurried to answer it, couldn't negotiate the doorway and missed the call. Marie was phoning from Israel. In her message she said something about being interrogated by the police. Her voice was steady, tight and a little defiant, even triumphant. Marie belonged to a feminist group whose role in the peace movement was to offer support to the refuseniks, those young men and women who refused to be conscripted. I rang her back but she was already on the phone to someone else and it was late when I was able to talk to her. The police had summoned her to answer some questions; she'd spent five hours with them, replying to their questions truthfully and freely—"I've nothing to hide, done nothing illegal. Isn't this still a democratic country? For some of us anyway"—and eventually they let her go. "They hated me," she said, that's what struck her most, the hatred she perceived in the two young Israeli policemen who questioned her. Hatred of her political views, hatred of intellectuals, above all hatred of women, especially radical intellectual women.

OUTBURST

Over two years into our sessions, I at last spoke out, and just the fact of doing so was a source of pride. But my notes are sparse, as if I was too shocked to retain a memory of our telephone exchange. I remember this much of the doctor's response to my outburst: "You can't go round accusing people," he said. And: "I vigorously deny ..." Also: "You imagined it ... wishful thinking." His anger, then—to which I responded with a cry: "I knew this would happen," though I didn't, and a pause I heard as a gulp, as he remembered himself and became conciliatory: we'd talk about it at our next meeting, keep to the rule of speaking only face to face. So a few days later, after I'd sat down and he'd waited as usual for me to start, I admitted my outburst had been aggressive, regretted my loss of control. But I was careful not to concede what I didn't believe, that I had imagined his seductive gaze. This, the doctor would always insist, was my misunderstanding, my seeing what I wanted to see, my delusion. Victor was of the same opinion, that the doctor couldn't possibly have acted as I said, and in any case it was a trivial enough offence. "Can't you laugh?" he asked. He also reminded me that I'd told him about it only retrospectively, many months later, as if it was the transposition of an earlier feeling into an after-memory of something that had been desired but hadn't in fact happened at all. I protested that I hadn't told him because I thought he'd want me to stop seeing the doctor—or perhaps because I hadn't at the time faced up to my feelings for him. Victor didn't understand my point of view, that it wasn't the doctor's actions that upset me but his refusal to talk of them, his denial. It was a shock that Victor didn't believe my account, that he sided with the doctor out of some instinct for solidarity with a fellow male, but I didn't argue.

We treated one another with exceptional care at this time, aware perhaps of the fragility of ours as of any relationship. He no longer joked about my crush on the doctor. Whenever the subject came up with friends who had their own good doctors he asked about their feelings, and was relieved when they described a preoccupation much like my own. "Still, I wish you could put it all behind you," he said. I wished I could too.

Certain things changed at the good doctor's, presumably to avoid further misunderstandings on my part. He adopted a new choreography for my departure after a session. He would remain in his chair until I had crossed the room and reached the door, when he would leap to his feet and back away from me as far as he could into the opposite corner. Also, he no longer helped me on with my coat, though I always struggled with it in the characteristic Parkinsonian way. At about this time too he told me a story, a sort of misogynistic moral tale, about a woman patient who seduces her male analyst, breaking down his resistance and forcing an affair, which the doctor in due course regrets and withdraws from. The woman, hell-bent on revenge, reports him to the authorities. He told me this story several times, often enough for me to wonder if he identified me as such a woman and was warning me off.

DEEP BRAIN STIMULATION

The question of surgery arose. An operation might help with certain symptoms of my illness and, if it worked, make me less dependent on drugs, thereby reducing their side-effects. At the hospital they explained how it would be. Leads implanted in specific areas of the brain are connected via extensions to a battery-run device placed under the skin on the chest. The device delivers electrical stimulation to the targeted areas to counteract the abnormal nerve signals that cause the symptoms of Parkinson's.

It's not a cure, this operation, and there are unwanted side-effects, notably damage to speech and language. Everyone had an opinion on whether or not I should put myself forward for this procedure, advocates like my friend Tina—"I'd have it like a shot, I wouldn't hesitate"—and those who regarded it with horror as an invasion of the brain. Victor said that to find it more difficult than I did already to retrieve words would seem like a wilful silencing of myself. The good doctor refrained from giving an opinion.

Later I would ask myself why exactly I hesitated. Rather than doubts about its efficacy and side-effects, could it be that I feared an amelioration of my symptoms? I had made my peace with the illness, having accommodated it within my life. In return it had allowed me to live as I wanted, to indulge my fearful preference for a quiet, undemanding existence, was in fact the perfect alibi.

DISCONSOLATE

A deep seam of discontent opened up in me and attached itself to a conviction that Victor and I should move house. Compulsively I read the estate agents' lists on the internet, but the houses and flats that were both better than ours and affordable were always far away from the centre of town. Victor had decided to humour me but was irritated every time I came up with a possibility. One flat in particular appealed to me, in a Victorian mansion block in Forest Hill. It was on the first floor and had high ceilings and the original wooden floors and shutters. There were four bedrooms—more than enough for Victor to house his library and have a studio— and an open fire in every room; its exceptional spaciousness was a draw, as was the balcony off one of the rooms, which I imagined as mine. Unfortunately, Victor didn't want to live in south London, wouldn't be persuaded, even of the attractions of a converted shoe factory in Camberwell, extending at the back into a long garden, with a series of inside-outside spaces. I tried Dalston, a ground-floor flat in a fine modernist block: again, spacious with several bedrooms, and very light. And also, more remotely, a glorious seventeenth-century house in need of restoration in Lincolnshire. I shouldn't have told Victor about that one—it persuaded him I'd lost touch with real life. But the main plank of his counter-argument was that where we lived now I had everything set up for my likely eventual decrepitude—a good GP's surgery round the corner, the hospital very close, accessible shops, and cafés and restaurants galore. I knew that we wouldn't move, I didn't really want to, but I went on searching the lists and dismaying Victor with my finds. Where did my restlessness, my discontent come from?

I stood in my room one day in front of a shelf of books by and about Isabelle de Charrière, who had meant so much to me when I first showed signs of illness and fled my life in London for an island far in the north. Belle had travelled in the opposite direction, from her provincial home to Paris, and she left her husband. I hadn't wanted to leave Victor. I wanted him to flee with me—as I did now, to go to a place where Parkinson's couldn't find me and all would be well. The gratitude I'd felt for years after Victor came into my life had survived the diagnosis of disease, but it had faded under the good doctor's scrutiny. He laid bare in me a dislikable negativity. I had lost my way to making the best of things, which was confused in my mind with my aim to stand up for myself, not to be brow-beaten, as if one couldn't do both.

In notes that are thin but at least legible I recorded a long period of repetition and monotony. "A bad meeting," I read on the screen. "I take to the couch, but I want to engage with the doctor. I want to see him and know his responses. *I love him.*"

"Another bad meeting," according to an entry a week later. "*I love him, but I feel he's withdrawing.*" Under the same date I also find several drafts of a fictional eulogy for a young girl killed at an early age in an accident. I seem to be as a mother to the child, since the death of her actual mother, my great friend. There's also a father, grief-stricken, and in a slightly ambiguous relation to me. We both adored the dead child but there's a sense that the ground has now been left clear for me, with nothing, or no one, to hinder our relationship, the father's and mine. I seemed to be intent one way or another on possessing a father—having first killed off the mother/wife and my child self who I'm tearfully eulogising.

"Yet another bad meeting"—triggering a storm of emotion: jealousy, sexual longing, and a painful tension. It was as if my brain was seeping into my body and poisoning it. I could hardly bear to wait a week before seeing the doctor again. But I did bear it, only to learn as I was about to set out for our session that he was ill. Victor took his call. Something was wrong, he didn't know what, but he was going to the hospital and couldn't see me. I tried not to show my anguish but I felt sick with shock and foreboding. Convinced he was dying, I was devastated by grief and feelings of loss. I had often imagined and dreaded the end, my departure after the last session of all: how I would glance back as I opened the door of his office, to take in his face, to imprint it finally on my memory—but then wouldn't be able to see him for the tears in my eyes. How at the bottom of the stairs I would again look back to see him standing at his threshold to watch me go. Would he lift his arm in a final salute, or turn his back at once and retreat? As I shut the door behind me, hardly knowing what I did, I'd remember all the other times I'd left him with a week to wait till I saw him again. How long those weeks were! But not as long as always. For ever. Without ceasing. Never, ever again. These are the words that would repeat in my mind as I walked, sobbing, along his street, which I'd never have reason to walk along again. "Never, never, never, never."

He recovered and within weeks was back in his office and our meetings started again. In the meantime I'd sent him a fulsome get-well card with references to his wisdom and goodness. A list of my much rehearsed resentments would have been a more honest communication. That he denied my reality when he didn't like what I was saying, and looked forbidding when he wanted to silence me. That he wouldn't be drawn on anything to do with his experience of our meetings. These complaints were amorphous, easily denied, and ascribed to my projection. At the same time I idealised him, hanging on to my idealisation as if it was a matter of life or death, as if he defended me against something, thoughts or feelings perhaps that were too terrible to know—like the mice I dreamt of, he would suggest, scampering around the periphery of my space, looking for weak spots in my defences.

COMBAT AND COMPLIANCE

The doctor said I arrived at each session with guns blazing and some complaint or other about something he'd said that I hadn't liked. "We're not," he said, "engaged in combat"—but I rather thought we were. The whole experience felt like a scrum, and it seemed to me that he frequently picked fights with me—possibly a strategy to galvanise me when our exchanges had become moribund and were in danger of grinding to a halt. Why do I always dwell on pleasant things and overlook the nasty? (He was referring to my omitting to mention the poverty and slums in Naples after a visit there.) Why do I always follow Victor's lead in travel? (Apropos a series of dreams of vehicular disasters.) Why does he have to wrench out of me any account of my feelings? (My delayed admission that I was hurt by his hectoring tone; my general tendency to be slow in response.) He thought my introversion hampered my creativity: "There are so many wonders in the world to write about but all you can think of is yourself." He complained that I read books that were out of date when I should be keeping up with the new. "Here and now," he said, "that's what's important."

He pointed out that I ascribed attitudes to him that were actually not his but mine. He cited my belief (delusion) that he had looked at me leerily—the first time it had come up since the day I named it. Perfectly composed, he insisted that it was my invention. I looked up some studies of delusion and saw that it could have been so, that what I thought was his acting out might have been my misperception and it was precisely in insisting on my rightness that my delusion lay. I began to feel stupid and stubborn, as if I was arguing my case against all the evidence and simply for the sake of opposing him. And though I could not conceive of myself as someone who did things she wasn't aware of doing, it came to seem childish to make such an issue of it. What did it matter? This, I always came back to: my extreme over-reaction not to his stares but to his ceasing to stare, what I perceived as the withdrawal of his feeling for me, that's what made me angry, that he had seemed to offer love and then to renege on his offer without a word of explanation. I was repeating with the good doctor a structure for relationships with men that I'd learnt early. It occurred to me then that to accommodate him would be to signal my strength, not my weakness. The doctor made much of the idea of psychological truth—that my misperception of his stares, say, was truthful in the context of my psychology, and that's what we were attending to, not the actual course of events. And then I felt mortified at the impudence of my accusation and sent him a note of apology. I saw where I was heading: self-abasement, taking responsibility so as to deflect the other's anger; then disgust with myself because compliance was the easy way out. But I gave up my intransigence knowingly; if I hadn't there could have been no way forward.

In a dream I see myself, in quarter-profile, at the bottom right-hand corner of the picture, watching a figure coming towards me. He—his gender would not be in doubt apart from his having an hour-glass waist, which I note in the dream as being like a woman's—is bandaged from head to toe, his whole body shrouded like an ancient Egyptian mummy. The bandaging is brightly, variously coloured to make a striped effect, and there would be nothing menacing about him were it not for his eyes, like thick-lensed goggles, and the implement he wields in his right hand—not a knife, more a pair of kitchen tongs, the kind that are used to serve spaghetti; in his other hand, like a waiter, he balances a tray of rectangular boxes containing, I suppose, whatever I believe he's about to insert into me. I might have expected this to be a frightening dream, but the weary "*Stop it!*" that I woke myself up with just sounded impatient—as if I was familiar with this ambiguously gendered person and he represented some concealed aspect of myself, a male aspect, that slightly bothered me, and I wished would go away. It occurred to me, as I considered it over the next weeks, that the figure in my dream was going to extreme lengths to tamper with me without touching. What the doctor called the non-touch technique, said to be safe for both parties.

By conceding the doctor's view of our interaction I hoped I would open up to him; rather, it intensified my inhibition, as if I'd robbed myself of the very matter I had to confide. Every meeting triggered a day of sadness made up of loss and dis-appointment. Anger would engulf me, and in these moods I blamed the doctor for the barrenness of my love. He saw my continuing attachment to him as infantile, a childish habit, and for me it was as if he was entangled in the knotted strings that were my relations with my parents. No "cure" was possible for this entrapment, and while I hoped my parents would recede, taking their place more peacefully in my memory than they had before, the doctor, or my feelings for him, which belonged to the present, here and now, held them back with the deaden-ing hand of my neurosis.

SOME THINGS GOT BETTER

At a reception for a visiting German artist, I enjoyed myself as I never had before at a formal social event. I remembered the private views Victor and I went to when we were first together, how tense they often were. But we were young then, and much of the tension came from being among older, more successful people and feeling intimidated and not wanting to appear to be on the make. Now we were the older ones, and I felt more confident, caring less what other people thought of me, readier to show my hand and let them know who I was.

Victor wore his only suit, with a collarless shirt (red), so he didn't have to wear a tie. I put on the outfit I always wear when called upon to look my best. Made of parchment silk, in a shot greenish bronze colour, the dress has a slightly fitted top. I love the luxury of the material against my skin and the softly crunchy sound it makes as I walk. It's almost worth the strain of a party to be able to wear it—and so that evening started well for me. It was pleasant wandering round the galleries, looking at the grand pictures, and greeting friends and acquaintance. There was a benign atmosphere. We felt good about ourselves and so did the people we talked to. There was little edge, and rather than criticise the paintings, as artists often did before the work of a successful contemporary, they were mostly admiring, and a few spoke of finding the pictures inspiring. It was very rare for me to leave such an event feeling liked and appreciated, and myself affectionate towards people I had long regarded as simply acquaintances.

The reception persuaded me that I'd gained enough detachment to understand the shape of things, and consequently to see the doctor for what he was rather than how my conflicted needs required him to be, to respect his manifest gifts but not to idealise or hate him, to admire his warmth and dedication rather than despise what I saw as his lapses of judgement, to feel fondness for him rather than desire—in sum to see him as a human being rather than as god or devil. It all seemed to take on a different complexion. I began to understand that my view had been inflexible and simplistic, that when the doctor made a distinction between something having an effect on later events and something causing them he was suggesting a complexity in explaining emotions that was truer than my idea of myself as victim of parental thoughtlessness and the patriarchy. It was likely that the snags in my construction were the result of phylogenetic factors as much as my father's excess of feeling and my mother's insecurity, and that the passion I had felt for the doctor was partly an effect of drugs.

RELAPSE

B ut then my new-found stability collapsed about me. A man, a stranger, stood at the doctor's front door as I turned in at the gate. I took in the situation—another patient was usurping my slot and I hurried up the path to stake my claim. The doctor looked crestfallen at finding two of us on his doorstep ("I think I've made a muddle") and while he sorted it out I waited in the living room and looked around me at the signs of his family life—photographs, a violin in an open case, an upright piano, newspapers, and a cat sitting on the table and gazing out of the window. It dawned on me, with a painful stab of jealousy, that the doctor had a whole life, filled not just with other patients, but with wives and children, and friends, and cats and dogs, and for hours of every day, and whole days of every week, I wasn't in his thoughts at all. He, by contrast, was never out of mine, even now, but not any longer as a lover. I would picture him eating his lunch or talking to his daughter over tea; or I would come upon him in some distant place, in the company of his family, and I'd assist them in some vital way, and they would take me to their hearts.

Sadness gripped me as I again contemplated the inevitable, that once I'd stopped I would never see him again. It would be as if he had died—and in the days that followed, by way of association, memories of my already dead haunted me. I found myself dwelling on the manner of their passing, and on my inadequate response. I had fled death, failed out of fear to help and support in extremis those I loved. I thought of my mother, unconscious on her death bed, and how I hadn't wanted to see her. My father persuaded me, said I'd regret it if I didn't, and so I stood at the foot of her bed, heard her slow, long-drawn-out breath full of effort and suspense. I couldn't bear to go any closer, couldn't bear to stay—and left.

ENDING

I described to the doctor the stuckness of my feelings for him, and my view that I could only neutralise those feelings by removing myself, that I wanted to bring our sessions to a close. He easily persuaded me that I wasn't yet ready to stop, with a harangue that was so extreme as to be comic. "Sure," he said, "if you're happy with yourself, if you have no urge to change aspects of yourself, then stop coming here." He said I seemed to be deeply distrustful of him, that I challenged his appraisals of my character as if I wasn't interested in what he had to say. He found me aggressive, he said, and yet he also claimed I was anxious to please him (even if failing spectacularly). The middle-class mores of my upbringing trapped me—oh, and also, he judged me "corrupted" by my reading of books on psychoanalysis.

I got it into my head that the doctor was having the same pernicious effect on me as Adrian, the object of my obsessive love in my twenties, that he was trying to turn me against myself, by challenging my perceptions, my sense of myself and my reality. I felt he was ill-intentioned, out to titillate his own desires, and to control and manipulate me. I wept at the failure of our interaction, at how an anomalous affection had obstructed any possibility of true empathy between us. It was like boxing with a shadow, the way I circled him trying to find a weak spot where he would admit his feelings. I was no longer possessed by the fantasy of mutual love but the corner of my brain that it occupied couldn't throw it off, my rational mind was no match for its tenacity.

Within a matter of hours I perceived the madness of my train of thought. This was paranoia, the belief that the doctor, rather than wanting the best for me, was enforcing his power over me by manipulating my emotional dependency on him. The morning after this realisation I woke feeling cleansed and renewed, somehow lighter and with an unfamiliar relish for my life. No longer uncertain, I resolved to end our meetings, and when I told him I said my decision was definite and final. His response was subdued. He didn't argue, simply asked if I was sure and, after a pause, what thoughts and reflections had led me to my decision. I said I believed I'd got as much as I could from our meetings, which was already a great deal. I cited my sense of coming more fully into myself, that the way I appeared chimed more harmoniously with my inner self—a process I expected to continue after I'd stopped seeing him. And I wanted too to re-engage with my life, and especially with Victor, for whom emotionally I'd been only partly present for far too long. I went on to explain my thought that my desire for him, the doctor, was a fantasy, just as the infantile state of mind it repeated had been. Perhaps my view of the doctor was itself also a fantasy. A friend who read this account commented that the good doctor was in some indefinable way absent from it. "He's not vivid," she said, "but it sounds as if in fact he was charismatic." How do you define someone who won't be known? The facts of whose life can only be guessed at? It occurred to me that my good doctor was absent because he was a creation of my obsession, a ghost that rattled its chains in a show of dynamism but actually was dead.

I began to see how little he had to do with my anger, that the aggression and hostility I expressed were directed at him as proxy for my father, and that, despite my complaining, and my ambivalent love, he had kept his head, and patiently, steadily, and often kindly too, steered me towards some kind of resolution—not a happier person, nor a nicer one, but braver and unillusioned.

The sun was beaming down on him through the window, and he seemed to be struggling to keep his eyes open. His breathing changed to a soft, steady whine that might become a snore, and as he nodded off his chin dropped to his chest. I too sank into myself, into a reverie, and found myself staring into a distinct rectangular space that somehow held everything that had occurred between us. Slowly, the rectangle, at first stark and angular, turned into a theatre: red plush, a proscenium stage, but with the lights dimmed. The performance was over, the audience had gone home, apart from a few chatterers who lagged behind, and a man who sat alone in the front row and appeared to be asleep. His head jerked forwards, and he woke with a little grunt of surprise. He sat up, and I saw that it was the doctor—manager of my one-woman re-enactment of uncertain memories—coming back into focus in his chair across the room.

ACKNOWLEDGEMENTS

Thanks to Timothy Hyman, who read and responded to the many drafts of this book.

And to Lyndall Gordon, a generous and illuminating reader.

To my writing comrades, Carolyn Polizzotto, Mirjam Hadar Meerschwam, and Rasaad Jamie, for their stalwart belief.

Tess Jaray, who enabled the book's passage into the world.

Richard Zimler, for his courage and his good heart.

My brothers Christopher, David, and Timothy, and my sister Ginny, for listening. And my cousin Annie Wattles, who shared all she knew.

Also to Gabriel Josipovici, for opening many doors to wonderful books. And, not least, Paul Becker, Carole Berman, Louise de Bruin, Dinah Casson, Elizabeth Claridge, Liza Dimbleby, Kate Foley, David Hass, Emily Maitland, Gina Medcalf, Miranda Miller, David Mitchell, Claire Peasnall, John Peasnall, Patricia Potts, Marianne Rist, Meg Rosoff, Carole Satyamurti, Helena Simon, and Tamar Wang. Dear friends, all.

ABOUT THE AUTHOR

Judith Ravenscroft was born in 1947 and grew up in Hampstead, London. She studied History at London University and became an editor of academic books and of Shakespeare. She started to write fiction after meeting her partner, Timothy Hyman, a painter. Her stories have appeared in various magazines and have won prizes, most recently for her writing about Parkinson's. She was diagnosed with the disease in 1997, aged fifty.

01432 560017